# SHUTT

By Cody F. Fonseca

For
Summer, Kayla, Elijah, and Helena Fonseca

Book Illustrations by Cody F. Fonseca
Book Cover art by Yocla Designs

CreateSpace Independent Publishing Platform
2015

Special Thanks to:
Abel "Sonny" Fonseca, Matt Brown, Darlene Owens, and Jojo
England for taking the time to proofread my story.

## Contents

Chapter 1 .................................................................9

    The King Sits ........................................................9

    To Be a Fool .......................................................10

Chapter 2 ...............................................................15

    The King's Legacy ..............................................15

    Bread of Life ......................................................16

Chapter 3 ...............................................................23

    A Servant Woman and Hope ...........................23

Chapter 4 ...............................................................33

    A Witch Among us .............................................33

Chapter 5 ...............................................................49

    A King's View .....................................................49

    Fool's Gold .........................................................51

    Journey Ahead ..................................................53

Chapter 6 ...............................................................61

    Fallen Man .........................................................61

Chapter 7 ...............................................................71

    Into the Forest ...................................................71

    Dream .................................................................79

Chapter 8 ...............................................................85

A Greedy Scheme ...................................................85

Journey's End ......................................................89

A Heavy Heart.....................................................93

King's Wrath .......................................................96

## Chapter 9 ...............................................................105

A Child Arrives ...................................................105

Plan for Revenge ...............................................110

Reveal.................................................................113

Eight Years ........................................................121

## Chapter 10 .............................................................127

Humble Home ..................................................127

Waking Up .........................................................131

Blue Moon .........................................................137

## Chapter 11.............................................................142

Firstborn ...........................................................142

Path ...................................................................148

Inside the Monster ...........................................154

## Chapter 12.............................................................157

An Old Woman's Offering .................................157

## Chapter 13.............................................................167

Safe Place ..........................................................167

## Chapter 14 .............................................................178

Sparrow ..................................... 178

Always a Fool ............................. 184

Into the Water ........................... 189

## Chapter 15 ................................... 192

The Husband/The King ............... 192

Promises .................................... 201

## Chapter 16 ................................... 209

Strong and Courageous .............. 209

## Chapter 17 ................................... 215

Light vs. Dark ............................. 215

Fair Warning .............................. 219

To the Death .............................. 226

## Chapter 18 ................................... 236

Killing Fields .............................. 236

Shepherd ................................... 239

Through the Fog Together ........... 244

One Last Time ............................ 247

## Chapter 19 ................................... 249

Together ..................................... 249

A Mother's Love ......................... 253

## Chapter 20 ................................... 260

Witness ...................................... 260

Friend .................................................... 264

## Chapter 21 ............................................ 269

Always Greedy .................................... 269

## Chapter 22 ............................................ 277

Call to Arms ...................................... 277

## Chapter 23 ............................................ 292

Brother ............................................... 292

Fishers of Men .................................. 298

Enemy of Mankind ......................... 301

## Chapter 24 ............................................ 305

Confirmation .................................... 305

Battle Lines ....................................... 309

In the Middle of the Fight ............. 312

## Chapter 25 ............................................ 317

Two Kings go to War ....................... 317

Master's Voice .................................. 323

In Good Company ........................... 328

## Chapter 26 ............................................ 332

Establishing Hope ........................... 332

Tree of Life ........................................ 335

# Faith

The King

# Chapter 1

**The King Sits**

The King sat on his throne, as he did every day that same hour. He would sit and stare. Before him was a temple built in his honor. It was an impressive monument, covered with elaborate images fashioned in the finest gold, which depicted the King's many victories in battle.

Regardless the urgency of any situation, the King demanded this time of reflection remain undisturbed. It was his time to contemplate his greatness as King—a time to remind himself of his vast power, his sovereign rule, and his enduring legacy.

Now, in his old age, he also needed this time to feel young and alive again.

"Oh, how I envy the days of my past," he said to himself.

The hour was almost up and, as was his custom, the King walked over to embrace the temple whispering,

"I see my life before me: yesterday, today, and tomorrow."

After giving his image a kiss he descended to the King's Hall.

## To Be a Fool

The King's Hall abounded with entertainers. There were dancers, musicians, wizards, and performers reenacting stories of old—stories of the King. Their sets were elaborate with extraordinary and outrageous costumes. Of all of the players, the King gave greatest authority to the Fools.

In the minds of most, being a Fool was both admired and feared. Fools were admired because they had sole responsibility for keeping the King entertained. They were also charged with assembling and training many of the performers.

The Fool himself must be well versed in every form of entertainment. When the quality of a performance fell short, it was up to him to step in quickly and bring it back to a level the King would find acceptable. If successful overseeing the King's entertainment, the Fool was handsomely rewarded, not only with lavish gifts but also with the respect of all the merchants and performers.

A Fool's position was feared, however, because the cost of failure was extremely high. Failure to entertain the King meant either a mark on the forehead and exile from the Kingdom, or—depending on the severity of the offense—death.

To be a Fool took much more than mastery of all forms of entertainment. A Fool also needed confidence, charisma, leadership skills, and most importantly, a sharp mind. The most talented Fool would be able to convince the King he was entertained even when a performance was poor. With a sly tongue and the shrewdness of a snake, there had been none better than Greedy Fool.

Every Fool was named by the King. Greedy Fool had come from a long line of Fools. His father, Angry Fool, was named for his intensity when preparing or rebuking the other players. This alone was entertaining enough for the King who rather enjoyed the abuse coming from Angry Fool. His reign as the King's Fool had never been matched before. Due to his intensity, and the stress along with it, Angry Fool was destined for a short life. He managed to die peacefully in his bed muttering the words,

"I'll kill...I'll kill you if you don't get it right."

Greedy Fool was given his name by the King because of his greedy nature. After the death of Angry Fool, the King sought a suitable successor. To gain favor with the King, Greedy Fool manipulated and sabotaged his rivals. This was to the King's liking.

# The Queen

# Chapter 2

### The King's Legacy

Twenty long years passed since the Kingdom was threatened with war. Even longer, still, was the Queen's desire for a child, but her hopes remained unfulfilled.

"I will go to my grave before I see an heir to my throne!" The King would argue.

"Then who will rule the people and carry on your legacy?" She would ask.

"My physical body may die, but my name will live, and it alone will rule the people. That is my legacy. The very fear that weakens their knees at the mere suggestion of my wrath will keep them obedient for years to come. As long as my temple stands, the people will continue to worship *and* fear me. Everything will be done 'by order of the King.' I will leave decrees to be carried out for years to come. When all those orders are fulfilled, they will simply begin anew, and so on and so forth. Stories will continue to be told about my greatness. They must. For if any of my old enemies, children of those I have put to the sword, hear of my demise, they will take back all they lost and will not look kindly on those who serve me. The Kingdom cannot carry on without my name or all will be lost."

Her pleas and tears were no match for his contempt and stubbornness. Still, even in her old age, she pressed the King. As the years passed, the Queen held on to the hope of carrying a child—a child of her own.

"Even if it shortens my life, if death can be put aside, even if only for a moment," she vowed to herself.

**Bread of Life**

On occasion, the Queen felt the need to sneak away to be amongst those she had known well long ago.

She was very good at disguising herself and blending in among the villagers.

On one particular day, disguised and wandering through a beaten path between the edge of the forest and the marketplace, she came across a little boy who appeared to be selling bread. This child was alone and unfamiliar to her.

"Where are your parents?" The Queen asked.

"I've got none."

"Well, where do you live? Do you not have any family?"

"No, I've no family here. I've a place in the forest."

"In that dreaded forest?"

"Yes, yer majesty, in the forest."

The Queen was taken back by his response. How could this child have known who she was?

"My dear boy, why do you call me 'majesty'?"

"I know you, my Queen. Our meeting is not by chance."

"Do you mean you are meant to sell me a loaf of bread? If I am in fact the Queen, then you know I am not in need of it."

"It is as you say. However, this is no ordinary bread. This bread is meant to bring you life…the life of a child…a child of your own."

The Queen gasped. She was certain her conversations about having children with the King were private. The boy should not have known about them. What's more, it would be unnatural to suggest a woman her age could possibly have children."

"Who are you and what do you know of such things?" She asked.

"I am only a messenger, yer majesty."

"A messenger of whom?"

"Someone aware of your distress. He has been eager to help you for some time, only, you weren't looking until now."

"Tell me child, who is this someone?"

"Hope."

"Hope?"

"There is little time, yer majesty. You must know that eating this bread comes at a cost."

"If it truly does as you say, then I shall pay any price. I have more than you can make in ten lifetimes."

"You may, but neither riches nor possessions are asked of you. It is your very life."

"How do you mean child?"

"It will be as you vowed, 'death will be put aside, if only for a moment,' so that you may have your child. However, you will not raise it nor see it grow. The agony of childbirth will be too much for your body and you will meet your end, but not before holding your child."

The Queen did not have much time to consider what she heard. The boy continued,

"If you refuse, you will live a much longer life, but you will never have a child. If you take this bread, you must eat it tonight, for tonight your husband will lay down with you for he knows your body has passed its childbearing age. In fact, your womb has been shut for some time because of the poisons he has secretly been giving you."

The boy quickly handed the bread to the Queen and before she could respond, he ran into the forest.

Back in her bedroom, the Queen stared at the bread and contemplated the cost of eating it. She considered her life and the life of her unborn child.

"Who would raise it? Who would love it? Surely, not the King. He will neglect it; maybe even put it to death. How long of a life would my child even have? Perhaps my child is meant for something great? But what? How do I choose? Do I risk the child facing the dangers of this world? Would this only be the result of my own selfish desires? Or, do I let this little miracle live a life it is possibly destined for?"

Many such questions continued to run through the Queen's thoughts. She was finally able to make her decision, however, when she envisioned holding her baby. She saw a child with her mother's eyes, with *her* face.

She envisioned this child growing up, taking its first steps, playing with other children. Boy or girl, it did not matter to her. She could hear the sound of her own flesh and blood, a child she dreamed about for countless nights, and knew it would be enough. She could see a warm embrace followed by a kiss. She took the bread and ate it.

She immediately felt overwhelmed with a sense of joy and began to praise Hope and whispered many times,

"Thank you."

That night, as the child foretold, the King lay down with his Queen. Death could not come too soon for her as she eagerly awaited the birth of her child.

# Chapter 3

### A Servant Woman and Hope

Not long after taking the bread, the Queen summoned a servant woman, one whom she had known for many years and found great favor in.

"Yes, my Queen?"

"You are to tell no one of this meeting, not even the King himself. Is this understood?"

"Yes, my Queen, with my life."

"Good, because it will be your life should you give in to the urges to speak foolishly or by some drunken stupor. I will have you sentenced to a hanging for blasphemy against me and your family will be taken far away, never to be seen again. Now, is *that* understood?"

"My Queen, yes, of course. You have known me since I was a child. You knew my mother; she was honest and raised me well. Please, let me assure you for I will not reveal these moments in a drunken state for I do not take to drinking nor take the liking to gossip. I am bound by my duty and honor to do as you say."

"Very well, we have no time to waste. What do you know of Hope?"

"Forgive me my Queen, for I do not fully understand..."

"Speak freely child, for I know about the stories told amongst the servants and their children. This is my castle and, unlike the King, I know everything that abides within these castle walls. This is no ordinary meeting. There will be no punishment for foolish stories here despite the King's orders against such."

"I am sorry, my Queen, but if it is your wish, then it will be so."

"Carry on child, what have you heard?"

"It is not so much as to what I have heard but, more so, what I have seen. As you know, your servants travel quite frequently to the market place for food and supplies. It is there where my story begins. As a child, I had always been fond of traveling to the market place because just beyond it is the forest. And there have always been many stories about it.

Many of the villagers call it 'The Forest of Ghosts.' However, they say it isn't just filled with ghosts and wandering spirits but with a winged creature they like to call 'Abaddon.'

People believe, when someone goes missing, it is because of Abaddon. Many are eager to avoid going into the forest, knowing there are dangers within. Still, they cannot help their curiosity. They lose themselves to the forest, as if something called them to it. He comes to take them away and feeds on them when animals in the forest become scarce. It is indeed a vile place, however, there is also a saying, 'Even in darkness, there is always Hope.'

No one has claimed to have seen Hope but know he's there because of his messengers. These messengers are said to be in the form of children, children lost to the forest long ago. Although, a merchant once told my mother he saw a messenger in the form of an eagle. He claimed to have heard it speak just as you and I speak now. I, too, believe I have seen one of these messengers. Oh…how you must now think I *have* before been in a drunken state."

"Not at all child, please, continue," the Queen reassured.

"Sometimes I consider if what I saw was true or not, and many times I think perhaps it was not. Some time ago, when I was still but a girl, I was with my mother and we were looking for choice meat for you and your King.

We came across an older man who we purchased from before. When I first saw him, he seemed uncertain of something. He didn't even notice we were there, standing in front of him when he said,

'Oh, my love, how I long for thee. Let this honey taste sweeter than the day I thee wed.'
In front of him was a spoonful of honey which he ate. Almost immediately, it seemed as if his heart was like that of a child again.

He looked over to his left where there sat a little dog. He smiled at it and said, 'thank you.' That was when he finally noticed us standing there and he said,

'What a glorious day to you and yours. Ye be my last customers for I am moving on. What shall it be? Anything you seek from me has no price. Tell me, what will you have today?'

He was very generous as he gave us much more than we had asked.

'Well, there it is. I'm off to join my love,' he said. 'I mustn't keep her waiting any longer.'
And at that moment, he turned and began walking into the forest with the little dog by his side. Now, I have debated this in my head many times but…I heard two voices, as if he was having a conversation with the dog. There were none else but them around.

What is even harder to understand is that I had known for some time, his wife had been long dead."

"My child," the Queen replied, "It is true as you say, for I too have been visited by a messenger of Hope. It is glorious, indeed, these feelings I now have, for although I am old in age, I will soon carry a child inside of me."

"My Queen, that is the most excellent of news. And this is because of Hope?"

"Yes, and while I eagerly anticipate the birth of my child, I have doubts about its safety."

"Doubts? Surely, a prince or princess of the King and Queen should not be short of protection, especially in these times."

"No child, you are wrong, for it is the King that I fear. He has made it very clear his wishes to remain childless. For many years, I have allowed myself the satisfaction of wishful thinking. The horrible truth is I have lost several children. I had always suspected it was my own husband using poisons against me, destroying my womb and any chance of having children. Now you see? I must hide the truth. Far be it from me to not give this child a chance to have a life of its own. If I must flee my Kingdom to have this child, I am prepared to do so. You must help me, for the life of my baby."

"Yes, of course. I am bound to you no matter the consequences."

The Queen and her maid servant devised a plan. The Queen was to hide her gain with extravagant dresses in such a way only a Queen could do. When the time was near to give birth, they would take a journey through the forest to the home of the maid servant's sister. It mattered very little whatever excuse the Queen would give to the King. He paid little attention to her, especially her whereabouts. Still, knowing the Queen would not return alive, they needed a convincing story to explain suspicious chatter.

"You will tell them we were attacked in the forest on our way back to the Kingdom," the Queen said. "Your sister must return with us so as to convince others the baby she carries is hers. This will be her baby. She and her husband will be taken care of for many years to come.

You must then tell them my body could not take the excitement of being attacked, thus, succumbing to my death."

"We shall be convincing to the end. None will be the wiser. However, there is one more thing I must tell you of the forest. There are, also, many stories of a witch."

# The Butcher

# Chapter 4

**A Witch Among us**

Villagers within the Kingdom had always known the stories about the forest, passed down for generations as warnings to their children. Many called it 'The Forest of Ghosts," or sometimes even, "The Forest of Lost Souls". People were terrified and dared not step foot into the dreaded forest alone. It was much easier to lose one's way than to find a source of light within.

However, long before the forest existed there sat in its place the best of all the lands: beautiful hills, green fields, and the riches soil. At the center of it was a flourishing town called Prosper. Many traveled from far away to enjoy the food Prosper had to offer. They were equally eager to barter for their healthy livestock. Prosper truly lived up to its name.

With the success of their land, and having been spared from any kind of famine or drought, the townspeople of Prosper were full of life. They would gather for many festivals and large feasts for any and all occasions. They had much in common and gave to one another as needed.

Chief among them was the Butcher. He was a natural leader of men; respected and admired for his wisdom and strong sense of morality. He took great pride in his ethic and unwillingness to compromise his beliefs. There was only one way of doing things, his way. The people wanted nothing less.

For many years, his wisdom was sought after by his fellow townsmen needing to settle disputes over trade, land, or even matters of the heart. Unfortunately, it was this very wisdom which brought about the fall of this great town.

One morning, the Butcher and his family were awakened by loud bangs at their door. Upon opening, he saw two men, both wide eyed and shaking as if they were cold or had seen a ghost.

"What is the meaning of this?" He demanded.

"Please, come quickly. We came upon something you should see. This could bring a disaster to our town!"

"Then show me at once."

The excitement of the men aroused others curious to see what the commotion was all about. Many even followed behind the Butcher. The men led him down a hill where they could see, at a distance, a small enclosed area of trees which had not been there before.

"Do you see there?" The men asked him.

"I see smoke arising out from the top of those trees. Is it a fire you are in fear of?"

"No, the fire burns…not of the trees, but from a small fire that sits in front of a house."

"And how can you tell there is a home dwelling within those trees. Even from our sights standing on this hill I see not a house."

The men were frozen and looked as though they were counting in their heads.

"I know not how those trees have appeared so rapidly," the Butcher continued, "nor do I know the one residing amongst those very trees. However, those are of little concern to me. What bothers me most is I do not yet understand why you have caused such a panic in our town. What is it you are so afraid of?"

"Please understand, if only under those circumstances we would not have bothered you at such an hour as this."

"Well then, on with it, what troubles you?"

"Please, again, understand if we ever had the slightest of doubt we would not make such an accusation as the one we are about to make."

"And you must understand that I do not take too kindly to anticipation such as this when there has already been enough build up to satisfy even the most single-minded of thinkers."

"Very well…there were not so many trees when we first saw them," they explained, "there were but only a handful. We could see the house and an oddness of sorts surrounding it. But now, it is overrun by trees. Brother, there is an evil among us! Living so near to our own homes, the homes of our families and dear friends, within these very woods you see before you is a home occupied by a witch."

"A witch!"

The townspeople in attendance all gasped at the same time.

"Yes, a heavy accusation this is," the Butcher explained, "one with the penalty of death by our laws should your accusation of witchery prove false! Are you sure you have considered the cost of what you are saying? Rest assure, if and when your speculation proves otherwise, prepare to be held accountable."

"By all that stands, we are fully aware and swear to it by our own children. We know this to be true."

"Very well, we mustn't wait any longer."

In no time at all, most of the townspeople arrived to witness the spectacle. What began as whispers quickly turned into loud outbursts and hysterics by different members of the community. Many feared, even speculated, but they found assurance in their leader.

Leading the way, like a Shepherd leading his flock, was the Butcher. He marched forward, eyes full of determination. The closer he approached the trees, the louder something inside of him screamed. He wrestled with his thoughts, trying to act as though his heart and mind were steady in dealing with such a wild notion as provoking a witch. He needed to look confident and strong for his people. They depended on him too much for him to waiver. Having played out different scenarios, he already decided what must be done, witch or not.

Standing at the foot of the trees, the Butcher closely examined them. With his eyes, he could count a hundred crows sitting on their branches deep within. *Their* eyes were fixed on the Butcher as if they were expecting him. With his ears, he could hear the trees stretching as they were growing before him. His feet could feel a small trembling. Roots were expanding underneath, as well as new trees beginning their ascent. With his hands, he felt the bark of the trees, their afterbirth still fresh. With his nose, he could smell a foul odor coming from within the tree line. He turned back only to see the rest of the townspeople standing far away in fear and awe.

He exchanged no words with them but simply gave a nod before turning one last time to face the trees. With his right foot he stepped forward, breaking the tree line.

Immediately, the crows were restless. They threatened an attack on the Butcher by swarming him violently, inches away from his whole body. They could have just as easily killed him if they wanted, but they didn't. Instead, they went back to their places on the trees. There, they could once again sit and watch the Butcher as he made his way in, letting him know he would be allowed to pass through. He took a deep breath before moving forward.

The air was thick, heavy. Fog rose from the ground continuously and with every step he took the forest expanded, as if it could be infinite. He realized it was no ordinary forest and magic must have had its hand in creating it. It was a place of its own, like another world.

Along the way, he heard what sounded to him to be a faint howl, a whimpering. He followed the sound and found a wild dog injured. Its leg looked twisted. Being a butcher, he was familiar with the anatomies of many animals. He wanted to examine the leg so he approached the animal slowly, trying to assure it of his intention.

The animal growled at first sight of him but was in too much pain to put up a fight. In its despair, it allowed him to examine its leg.

"With a couple of snaps, a splinter, and some time, this animal should indeed return to its natural state," he thought to himself.

He made two quick snaps producing a loud cry from the dog. The creature licked his hands to show its appreciation.

"Good boy," he said, "let me find something to mend this. Maybe we can even find a home for you."

The Butcher wandered off to find the right materials. While in search he heard several dogs viciously barking from the same direction as the wounded animal. He dropped what he gathered and raced quickly back to the scene. It was too late. Three other wild dogs stood over the lame one, digging their teeth into its flesh. There was no sense for him to try and break them up. The animal was dead and the moment was his chance to sneak away unnoticed by the other dogs.

Farther in, the air was colder and the crows, having been perched in their trees, were dropping dead one by one. Some of their bodies burst on impact, exposing the worms already inside of them feasting away. Another, and then more. Hundreds had fallen and not before long, the ground was covered by them. The Butcher had no choice but to walk atop the dead, rotting creatures.

He could smell smoke and knew he was close. This was the motivation he needed. However, his self-assurances were growing weaker by the distractions of the forest and the fears accompanied with them.

He took a deep breath again, trying to stay calm. Suddenly, a thousand voices screaming in agony surrounded him, coming from all directions. He heard cries for help and the sounds of a crackling fire. The Butcher, filled with panic, covered his ears and yelled as loud as he could in an attempt to drown them out, but they were too much to handle. The louder he screamed, the more the voices intensified. He picked up his pace and ran as fast as he could toward the smell of the smoke.

There were terrible things all around. In front of him were the haunting images of death. The dead spirits of the people he once knew, even those he knew to still be alive. They all screamed for him to save them. Their bodies were ghostly, almost completely transparent. They were disfigured having horrific scars and missing limbs.

The noise did not stop, and so he continued to run for what felt like the amount of time it would take to get to another village.

The ground shook violently with the screams as he came upon a dense fog. He was afraid of jumping through because he could not see anything visible beyond its outer wall.

He was out of options, trapped, surrounded now by the dead spirits and their pain. The ghastly figures approached him with their arms stretched out, still screaming in agony, pleading with him. He could not bear it any longer. There was no choice but to escape through the fog and face the unknown.

All at once, the voices stopped. The forest was silent. He stood for a short time, both relieved and worried, trying to catch his breath. It was as if all life froze around him. He feared for what other kinds of black magic the forest was bound to offer him. Still, he was not yet ready to admit defeat, nor ready to admit to his regrettable actions. There was no going back, his people depended on him too much.

The smell of the fire was undeniable. He knew he would stumble upon it any moment. He followed through the abyss, and before he could finally see the faint outline of a house, the fog slowly dissipated.

In front of him was a small and unimpressive fire, but the smoke rising from it was frightening. It was nothing like it appeared when he was at the top of the hill. Rather, it resembled a whirlwind spinning in all directions shooting straight into a night sky. There were flashes of lightning and the smell of burning sulfur coming from within. The heat given off was overwhelming.

Around the flame sat large stones, large enough for a person to lie down on. Although the Butcher entered the forest in the early morning he could see the constellations mapped directly above the house.

There was a clearing around unlike anywhere else in the forest. The moon was full and very bright. It all felt otherworldly to him. As if he was in a different state of existence. All he had known to be true was lost forever.

The house itself looked old and frail. The windows were open but there was only darkness inside. As he stood in awe of the sight, he could smell a faint odor. At first, he thought nothing of it until it started to sting with every breath he needed to take. He covered his mouth and nose as best he could. It did not matter. He looked for the source, but found nothing in front of him to be guilty of it. That is, until he looked down.

His feet were like rotted flesh inhabited by the worms and maggots of the earth. The Butcher tried in vain to shake off the insects. He reached down with his hands only to notice they were infected as well. To his horror, he could feel his face melting away. The man could no longer withstand the agony. His mind and body gave out on him.

As he lay on the ground, his blurred vision caught a glimpse of the door to the old house. It was open.

# Chapter 5

### A King's View

The King stood atop his castle, as was his custom, the same hour every day. He stared and examined what was before him, his Kingdom. Built and amassed by his great power, it was a large Kingdom, covering the known world and matched by no other in all the land before his mighty reign.

Erected throughout his Kingdom were gold images of himself with the stories of his victories engraved in all of them. The moment of reflection, like most of his days, were to be undisturbed, no matter the emergency. Nothing was more important to him.

It was his time to reflect. To think about how great a King he was; to remind himself of his power, his rule, and his legacy. As before, this was his time to feel young again, to feel alive.

"Oh, how I envy the days of past," he said to himself. "If only a new brash enemy would rise up and try to run me down so I could do battle once more."

Still, as it had been for many years, none would. There was never a King like him before. None were so powerful, so feared. He was the King of Kings. The fear he instilled in all the land drove other kings, lesser kings, to send over delegations asking for peace and pledging their allegiance.

In one of his battles long before, as many as four kings joined their armies and marched against him. They failed. With no enemies to challenge him, the King stood high above his Kingdom, yet, he was without peace. Something was missing. To fill the void, the King entertained ideas of instigating wars, small battles allowing him to lead a small group of men against a much larger group. He needed another Kingdom to conquer, even if he needed to travel to the ends of the world. What he had was simply not enough.

"Is it the excitement of having another man's blood on my hands I seek? Is it the roar of my Kingdom as I ride back in after victory? My Kingdom is perfect, any other King would be content with just a fraction of my power, but as long as I live, as long as I have breath within these bones, I will seek more. I am not like any other king. I am not worshipped as a man among men, I am a god!"

## Fool's Gold

Every Fool knew the risk, but they also knew: without risk, there could be no reward. Although Greedy Fool was handsomely recompensed for his work, by his nature, he could not resist helping himself to some of the King's gold.

The King was vastly wealthy. His combined fortune was accumulated by the many spoils of war, the taxes he collected, and the tribute offerings made in his honor. It was too much for 100 men to keep track of. Still, he expected every trinket of gold to be accounted for and this responsibility was and had always been appointed to the Fool.

Greedy Fool helped himself to the smaller pieces he knew the King overlooked and to compensate, he inflated the reported amounts. He avoided stealing the larger and more decorative pieces so as to elude any suspicion from the King.

Little by little, and with many months apart, Greedy Fool would amass his own treasure trove hidden away for safe keeping. He had many traits but second to greed was patience. He knew if he was patient enough he could leave the Kingdom for another and start a new life with titles and more land than he could dream of.

Greedy Fool wanted to be served and to live a life of pleasure, indulging in all of his fantasies. His favorite moments as a Fool were to look at the King's face when even the slightest of entertainment was displayed. He did this, not for the satisfaction of successfully fulfilling his task, but to capture what it could be like to have more...like a king.

## Journey Ahead

The Queen and her maid servant started making preparations for their journey. Eight months passed and the Queen's wardrobe had long been criticized in the dark. The villagers and servants were not sure if she had lost her sense of fashion. Her attire became increasingly more extravagant and overdone and they snickered when they saw her pass. Still, none dared to personally question her.

Unfortunately, her lavish new attire attracted the attention of Greedy Fool. He would count each gold trinket as she walked by him, readying his hands, eagerly anticipating one of them to fall off to be forgotten.

On the night the Queen was to leave, having already given the King an excuse to go away for a while, she left his side at the dinner table early. Greedy Fool knew the walking paths of the Queen as she was, like the King, a person of habit.

He followed her all the same, keeping a close eye on the ground she walked, until something unusual happened. The Queen did not make her way to her room for the night. Instead, she walked through the dark courtyard toward the servant quarters. It was indeed an odd moment as, like everyone else, Greedy Fool knew the King and Queen were never to be seen near the servant quarters. It had become against their custom and out of place by social standards.

He followed the Queen carefully at a safe distance, but he was no longer interested in fallen treasure. He was determined to know the reason for such a secret meeting. The Queen's maid servant had come out to greet her hastily and guided her inside. Greedy Fool searched endlessly for a way to spy on the assignation before he found a crack within the wood of a closed window.

There they stood, talking about traveling and making final preparations. The Queen, with the help of her maid servant, started to remove her outer garments revealing the secret he was looking for. The Queen was pregnant. There was no doubt in his mind she was with child but why, he wondered, had this been hidden from the rest of the Kingdom? His mind was restless. He wondered if even the King was made aware. He needed to know more.

He ran to the door and pounded on it with authority.

"Is there a maid servant here?" he shouted.

Both the Queen and her maid servant went into a panic.

"Is there a maid servant here?" he demanded again as he continued to beat the door.

"My Queen!" shrieked the maid servant, "What should we do?"

"Quickly," the Queen began, "hand me my…"

"I hear you in there! I'm coming in!"

He busted through the door.

"The King requires…"

"Ah!" they both cried out.

"Oh my, your majesty, I did not…"

Greedy Fool stopped short in his apology to play the part of a man surprised.

"My Queen, I celebrate thee! What a glorious occasion to see you with child."

"The only surprise," she quickly replied, "is your unwarranted entrance into this woman's dwelling. Have you no shame to enter without permission?"

"I am truly sorry your majesty, under any other circumstances I dare not enter in such a manner. However, the King urgently needs an extra hand and told me to be haste. As everybody knows when the King speaks so, we are to act accordingly and spare no expense. All is just for the King."

"Very well," the Queen responded, "it is as you say. But let me be clear and speak to you in such a manner you ought to brace yourself as a man. While what you see here is glorious indeed, it is of none of your concern, or anyone else in the Kingdom for that matter. Shall I hear you so much as incite a little thought or curiosity to my present state I shall have you tortured and executed in front of the entire Kingdom for treason and conspiracy to kill the King. Is that understood?"

"With all of my good health, yes, it is understood."

"Very well then, perhaps you shall go and find another maid servant as this one is unavailable."

"Yes, yes of course your majesty. I shall look for another and I shall keep my thoughts and words far from these events of now."

"That is wise of you."

Greedy Fool turned to the doorway as if to leave, but stopped short. He turned to the Queen for one more question.

"My Queen, if I may? Perhaps I can rejoice with my King privately as you wish to keep this a private matter?"

At this, the Queen had become enraged.

"Did you not hear my orders before? Do what you ask and I will make sure your death is slow and painful!"

"Understood."

Greedy Fool turned once again and quickly closed the door behind him.

"We must hurry," she told her maid servant. "We cannot depend on the word of a Fool."

"Yes, my Queen. I will prepare the horses and carriage and meet you out back."

The Queen put on older looking outer garments to avoid recognition on her journey. She made her way to the door and took one last deep breath. She left.

Abaddon

# Chapter 6

**Fallen Man**

The room was dark, cold, and wet. There was a foul odor in the air. His body was numb and his head felt as if it were spinning. So much so, he was barely able to turn over to vomit. Even then, he was hungry and he could feel his lips parched from thirst.

"Does that make you feel better, make you know that your insides have come out, out with the bad?" said a strange voice from what sounded like an old woman.

"Who are you? Where am I? What have you done?" asked the Butcher who tried in vain to see with whom he was speaking.

"One, Two, Three questions. You only get one, one at a time."

"Who are you?"

"Who I am is not that important, is it important? And I don't care who you are, you are no use to me yet, not yet. Who you are Mr. Butcher, it's not who you are but what, *what* is right."

"And what am I to you?"

"Cattle, Mr. Butcher. The same cattle you cut to pieces and feed to little children, feed the fattest ones."

The Butcher tried to shake away the haze in his eyes so perhaps he could see her. Although he was not bound to anything, he was unable to move. He felt as if something was weighing down on his every muscle.

"I know the thoughts in your head Mr. Butcher, your thoughts. You're a good man, by your standards. You want to know many questions about me, but soon they will not matter, no matter at all. You worry about those people standing outside my trees, some still there,

some home in their comfortable beds trying to forget,
dreaming of better things, trying."

"What is it you want?"

"I want what any person really wants…to live.
Live my life, my own, and I choose to live it here."

"It is settled then. You will live here on the land
your trees have over taken. Rest assured we will leave
you in peace."

The old woman gave a laugh which sounded more
like a shriek. The Butcher's eyes were disobliging. All he
could see was darkness; in the middle, a grey mist. It
hovered in what he could make out to be the center of the
room. In quick moments, he could see a shadow passing
through. He wanted to see the old woman with his own
eyes.

"You act as though you have all authority, act. But
you have none over me, not you. And I know what you

call me. I go by many names Mr. Butcher, but the one you are most familiar is witch. Though it is not my name but a moniker in which people like you name names to feel comfortable at night knowing there is someone or something worse than you living in this world, living among you."

"Whatever you are, I have no quarrel with you so long as you leave me and my people be."

"Would you have said the same if I was a frail old woman mistaken by two of your cowardly men to be a witch, the same?"

"No," he responded shamefully.

"Honesty. That is rare. Yes, you would have thrown me in the river, drowned. I saw your heart's intention the moment you stepped into my forest, the very moment. You had already decided what was to be done to me, you decided."

"It is as you say. I judged you unfairly. Please, forgive me."

"Yes, you judged and now you will be punished accordingly, punished. And forgiveness is not mine to give. That is for the children. Punishment is mine."

"No, please. Perhaps there is another way. My family…"

"Yes, and they too will be punished, they too."

"No! I beg of you, have mercy. Your quarrel is with me."

"So, which is it Mr. Butcher? Do we or don't we have a quarrel? You meant to do me a great deal of harm and so here I am offering you the same kindness in which you have shown me. I have placed judgment on you and your village without giving any warning or heeding any advice. They are to be condemned blindly."

"Please, I'm sorry!"

"Sorry? I don't care, 'sorry.' It is already decided. There *is* a reason you cannot move, Mr. Butcher, nor can you see in such a way you are accustomed to. I have sentenced you to a life continuing in your very nature, blind injustice, you are blind."

"I do not understand. So, you will allow me to live?"

"I do, understand, and so I will allow you to live but it is how you live in which you are to be punished. The reason your body is so heavy is because it is in fact, heavy. It is transforming, your muscles will sort themselves out soon enough, soon. What you see now is all you will see, darkness and shadow. Nothing more, nothing."

"What am I becoming, you fiend?!"

"Death, a creature of death. Soon you will eat the flesh of living creatures. Oh, perhaps your own children," she said with optimism. "As a leader of men, you will not do well to lead your family. Not in your state, not at all. You will not decide their fates, live or die, you will always choose death. Soon, when your body is ready, I will release you, and your hunger will take over. Your mind will not control what your body craves, its need to eat, your body. When your hunger strikes, it will feed and you will hear the death screams of those you love and there is nothing you can do to stop yourself from ripping them limb from limb, ripping."

"This is a penalty worse than death! Please, kill me now. That much I deserve."

"Yes, yes, it is worse, but you will serve me well making your dwelling in my forest, keeping out those that wish to do me harm such as yourself. And do not attempt the taking of your own life for you cannot die by your own hand or will, cannot."

The Butcher could no longer hold back his emotional agony. He wept. The pain set in. He could feel his body changing those very seconds; bones were breaking, making way for bigger and stronger replacements. His teeth fell, as each new tooth pushed their way out. They were larger and much sharper. His body suffered. His screams started to sound like that of an animal. Bat-like wings slowly tore through his back. He was becoming a new creation, a dark one.

Shortly after his conversion, she released him. He devoured almost all of those living in his village, including his family. He heard their pleas, cries for mercy. All he could do was try to explain to them. Tell them he had no control. Tell them he was not really a monster, but in their distress, their rationality was replaced with fear and terror. His new body was hungry. It needed to feed and it spared none. It listened to neither their prayers nor wishes. The Butcher was gone. Abaddon was born.

# Chapter 7

## Into the Forest

The Queen and her maid servant reached an entrance to the forest.

"Is there another way?" asked the Queen.

"No, your majesty. The forest is too wide to travel around. The journey would not be kind on you and the baby. It would neither be too good an idea to risk exposure as we pass village after village. Alas, fear not your majesty, I have traveled this path before and have learned of the secrets to a safe passage."

"Very well, my life and the life of my child are in your hands."

Before they set off, the maid servant reached into one of her bags and pulled out wild fig leaves. She placed them all over the chariot as well as the reigns of the horses.

"These will shield us from restless spirits and the dark magic."

Then she pulled out a jar of perfume, along with tiny mirrors. She poured some of the perfume on the head of the Queen, on herself, and then on the horses. Next, she carefully placed the mirrors on the wooded wheels.

"The perfume will ward off our scent from Abaddon and the mirrors will confuse our image from the rest of the evil lurking these woods."

"What is an Abaddon?"

"It is said, Abaddon lives within the forest and can never venture out. The stories passed down claim it was once a man, a man that once lived where the forest now sits. A village was overrun by the trees almost overnight. One by one, Abaddon attacked and killed the villagers. The few that managed to escape told of their horror. The creature, blind, eyes shut, seemed to attack uncontrollably.

They said the monster spoke as it tore through the flesh of its victims. They heard it plea for forgiveness and begged them to flee for their lives. Other stories say the creature shouted out for death, demanding for someone to kill it."

"This is a horrible story. Poor souls."

"Many believe the witch created the monster, but fear not, these anecdotes for passage have been used many years with success by many families such as mine. There is nothing to worry about as long as we stick to the path and apply what we've learned."

The chariot started its ascension into the dark, cold forest. As soon as the chariot broke the tree line, the Queen realized the moment marked the first time she was to be separated from her King. Even in his battles, he always had her near.

She liked to remember the better times they had together, the times before he became King. They talked many sleepless nights about having multiple children; who they would look like, and names they already picked out. She never imagined then how horrible he would become with just the thought of having a single child. While he was no longer the man she knew, she was still deeply in love with him. Having to leave was difficult for her. She would never see him again. She left knowing she would die.

On their last night together, the Queen wanted to sing to him in bed, the way she always used to, but the King did not acknowledge her. Instead, he suggested for them to sleep in separate rooms from then on. He seemed annoyed at her gestures of affection. There was no goodbye kiss, no final embrace, or any words of affirmation. She was out of his life forever, and he knew nothing of it.

The maid servant had her reservations about the journey, but made no mention to the Queen. Although she succeeded the trip many times before, something was different. She could sense the intentions of the forest. A cold wind blew through her and gave her a grave chill.

As she steered the carriage, a single crow flew within inches of her head. Back and forth, it went, before it finally perched on the yoke of the horses. It sat facing her, staring deep into her eyes and unmoved by the bumps in the road. She was certain the bird was smiling.

The maid servant was uneasy. It was unnatural, and the first time the forest made its presence known to her. Not long after, another flew back and forth, once again, within inches of her head. The maid servant held her breath and did her best not to scream. This bird found its spot atop the carriage over her left shoulder. She could feel it close.

As if to whisper in her ear, the second crow squawked while the other continued with its death stare. She could not give in. She took deep breathes and kept her eyes fixed on the road ahead, when suddenly, there was a small thump near her. Whatever it was, she could feel its movements as it crawled about. She could hear its little tick sounds with each step hitting the wooded surface. The tapping moved from the seat and made its way up the top of the carriage. The crows became uneasy and started flapping about. Their confidence was shaken; each gave a final caw before flying off.

The maid servant was uncertain how to feel about this creature. She imagined it to be a terrible looking spider, hideous in appearance and large. Still, there became a certain sense of calm over her body. Any other time before, the thought of her seeing a spider brought her chills. This was different. There was no fear, no panic, but a renewed mind.

*Tick, tick, tick*, as it crawled just inches from her head.

*Tick, tick, tick.*

*Tick, tick, tick*, and the sounds faded off to nothing. A messenger of Hope, she knew.

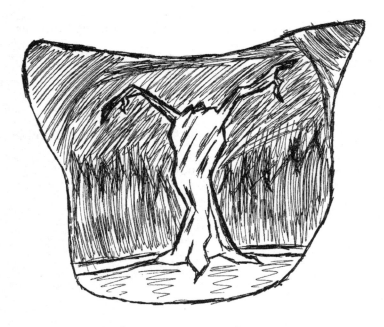

# The Dead Tree

# Dream

The Queen had been in a constant state of fear and anxiety since the first moment she knew she was pregnant. Her fears were not so much for her own life but, rather, the salvation of her child. She knew her momentary happiness would be considered a blessing, but a blessing with a heavy cost.

She questioned herself constantly. Was she being selfish? Would a life possibly filled with imminent danger be fair for a child to grow up into? While her thoughts ran circles in her mind, the Queen drifted off into a deep sleep. It was the first time she slept in many days.

This is what she dreamt:

The Queen awoke in the middle of the forest. She was cold, lost, confused. She did not know how she arrived there. It was dark, but if she looked hard enough, she could see light glimmer between the branches of the overcrowded trees. Enough light came through for her to notice footprints just ahead of her, walking along as if someone was there, a ghost perhaps, some residual entity reliving its past.

The Queen was more curious than shocked by the paranormal sight. She pursued them to see where the mysterious steps might lead her. She wondered if, possibly, they were there to guide her.

The footprints had a certain kind of character to them. They fumbled along, clumsy. Sometimes they would stop and then suddenly run, all in a moment's notice. She exhausted herself trying to follow. She needed answers so she contemplated the different ways she might communicate to whatever they were.

First, she tried to call out, but she had no voice. No matter how hard she tried, no sound would come from her mouth.

Her next approach was to throw any object she could pick up in its direction, over the footprints, expecting a thump as if to hit a person's back. Nothing. They continued their steps, and she continued to follow.

Out of the corner of her eyes, she noticed a shadow. Every time she tried to catch a glimpse of its movement, it was gone. Again, and again. These obscure stalkers surrounded her, but she could not see their source. There was no man or animal, no noise, just shadows. The Queen was frightened by them as they increased in frequency. The footprints she followed seemed frightened as well. They hesitated in deciding which direction they would go to retreat. First right, then stumbled, and turned to run in another direction before finally settling on a hidden, beaten path. The Queen, without hesitation, followed.

Still running, she ran as best she could trying to keep up with her invisible friend. However, the shadows could not be outrun nor hidden from. They fenced them in at every turn. Each path was blocked by darkness, and both the Queen and the footprints were trapped.

The shadows encircled them and slowly ate any remaining light. The Queen, knowing her efforts had come to an end, closed her eyes and was ready to let the darkness consume her. She braced herself knowing if they took her, she would be taken away forever.

It was in this moment time felt as if it had stopped. A bright light broke through the shadows in an instant, saving her and revealing her final destination. The light had overcome the darkness, slowly removing what was once there around her and changing it into something else. Like a layer of new paint stripped down to the original colors underneath.

She stared at what was before her: a circled courtyard, lit by firelight atop seven pillars. There were eight pillars total, but only seven were lit. At the center of the courtyard was a dead tree. The ground beneath it was charred, extended out as far as its remaining branches.

The footprints before her displayed an approach of uncertainty, but made their way towards it none the less. The Queen followed.

As she stared at the tree, she couldn't help but feel a certain sense of sadness. It was as if she knew the tree had a small amount of life left somewhere within it, but no one knew about it. How could they? She thought to herself. It was hidden away from the world, lonely.

The footprints made their way around the tree to the other side and came to a stop. The Queen approached slowly and noticed the footprints standing before a mirror leaning against the trunk. She stood side by side with her guide so she could stare at the same mirror. Staring back at her was her husband, the King, revealing the footprints were his all along.

He was worn down, exhausted, but in this moment, she knew he could see her. He cried out, sobbing. He was desperately trying to talk to her, but she could not hear him. The Queen could tell he was repeating something, over and over again. She cried and shouted out to him in vain.

The King reached his hand out to her, and as if he were passing through from another world, it made its way out of the mirror. In haste, she fell to her knees, frantic to take hold and pull him through. At the moment just before contact, she was shaken by a bump in the road, waking her up from her slumber.

# Chapter 8

## A Greedy Scheme

Greedy Fool was beside himself with such excitement it was hard for him to contain it. He giggled while he schemed for a mischievous way to use his new-found knowledge.

"Why keep this from the King?" he wondered. "Perhaps the child does not *belong* to him? Surely, the King will reward me for this information, maybe with a castle of my own? Still, I must be certain he would intend to keep it should it be his. What a marvel for the Queen at her age to even be with child, but if this is indeed a child belonging to a man other than the King, then this little marvel is mine in the form of riches."

In the middle of the night, the King was awakened by loud cries and moans. Peeking out of his window he saw Greedy Fool in the courtyard. He immediately sent a guard down to remove him so the King could go back to sleep. And it was so. The King rested without any more disturbance.

The next day, while the King sat on his throne to think of himself, he heard the familiar cry from the night before. It was, once again, disrupting him and he was greatly annoyed. He stood up from his throne and walked over to investigate. Turning the corner, he saw him again.

"Greedy Fool, what is the meaning of this childlike display?"

"My King!" he said with a surprised tone, "Please forgive my suffering, I dare not intend to disturb your time alone. I know how important it is to you."

The King scoffed at his response. However, he could not deny his curiosity.

"What is this suffering you speak of?"

"My suffering will bring great dishonor to my family's name. It is of a doing I wish not to speak to anyone about, but because you are my King, and you demand an answer, I shall give it:

My wife lives in a nearby village as I attend my duties here. After you ascended to bed this night's past, I made it a point to see her, being as it has been several months since my last visit. To my shame, I could see that she is now with child. However, I have not lain down with her for some time. She tried to keep the truth hidden from me by saying she has simply gained weight and nothing more. The type of clothing she wore was too large for her body, as if she was trying to hide it. I could not bear it any longer. I had her thrown into prison for her iniquities. It was only then did she confess to me her crime. Now, I am shamed."

The King paused for a brief moment before he replied, "Your duties to me are far more important. Do not let this interfere again."

"Of course, my King."

"Now, keep it quiet and make sure nobody else disturbs me."

"Certainly."

The King turned to escape back to his throne, but Greedy Fool was not finished.

"My King, before you go, may I ask for your wisdom in this matter?"

The King prided himself as a man of wisdom so he could not resist.

"Very well. Make it quick."

"If you had a child…"

"That is impossible!" he interrupted, "I do not and will not have a child. This is neither for you to ask nor suggest again or you will lose your place here and be banished forever to the forest!"

The King turned quickly one last time, without waiting for a response, and retreated back to his throne. Greedy Fool remained, once again, unable to contain himself.

## Journey's End

By the end of the three-day journey, the Queen could see the sunlight approaching ahead, finding its way through the dark forest. After they exited the last wall of trees, both the Queen and her maid servant had taken deep breaths of the fresh country air.

The Queen stretched her head out the window of the carriage to let the heat from the sun hit her face.

"It will not be much longer my Queen."

The Queen could not have felt any more pleased to hear those words. However, the pleasantry of the news was only momentary. She felt the sensation of water running down her legs. In a panic, she called out to her maid servant. There was no time to waste. The child was ready.

The maid servant commanded the horses to pick up their stride. They galloped with a new sense of purpose as if they understood their need to hurry. The home of the maid servant's sister was not much farther ahead, but to waste as little time as possible, she shouted out for her sister.

Her sister came out of her home and saw the horses approaching fast. Although they were still a long way off, she could see the terror in her face.

"We must hurry!" the maid servant shouted to her as they arrived. "The child is ready."

"So soon?" she responded in disbelief, "Something must be wrong."

The sisters helped the Queen off the carriage as she moaned in agony. After they entered the home, the maid servant's sister, as quickly as she could, prepared the bedroom for delivery.

"I'm sorry sister, my husband is away. Had I known the baby was coming so soon, I would have made the appropriate arrangements."

"We have no time to worry about that now. We will bring this baby into the world ourselves."

The pain of child birth was unlike anything the Queen had felt before. It was a very long and exhausting ordeal. Still, she never considered giving up. She gave every ounce of her strength for her baby. The source of strength was a picture she created in her head long before. An image she carried with her both day and night and even in her dreams: holding a child of her own, in her arms.

She persevered through her pain knowing full well it would come at the cost of her life. She pushed and pushed, until finally she heard the most beautiful sound, the sound of *her* baby's cry.

"Here she is my Queen. A beautiful baby girl," said the maid servant.

The Queen wept as her child was handed to her.

"She is beautiful, she is so beautiful!" the Queen cried out.

Her daughter gripped her finger tightly as she searched for the first taste of her mother's milk.

This was the Queen's moment. Even through her struggles, even as she began to fade, she knew it was worth it. The baby got her fill and had taken a gaze into her mother's eyes before falling fast asleep in her arms.

"She is my daughter, my beautiful baby, but you must promise me you will care for her as if she were your own and love her the way a mother should. Tell her stories of Hope. I want her to believe as I have come to."

"With all my heart," the maid servant replied. "Have you a name for the princess?"

"Yes. She shall be called Elise." The Queen turned her attention back to her child,

"My daughter, I do not know what troubles await you, but be strong and courageous. You will not be alone and your birth is not in vain. We will meet again someday."

The sisters cried as they beheld their dying Queen. They watched her kiss her daughter one last time before she slipping peacefully away.

## A Heavy Heart

The King slept-in, uncharacteristically. The last few days for him felt heavy. He turned over to feel the cold spot of his bed usually occupied by his wife, the Queen.

Having started his day later than usual, he set himself back from his normal routine which began a series of regrettable decisions. He was not happy about that. He was unable to take hold of his desire to start the day late.

As the King, he desired control over everything, especially with the menial tasks in his daily rituals, something he had given his life to with much discipline. Yet, things were different and they changed as if overnight.

His breakfast tasted bitter and so he replaced his head cook of over twenty years. He was enraged shortly after his impulsive decision because he then realized he would need to grow a new taste for another man's cooking. Once again, something he had been familiar with for many years changed. There was no going back on his hasty decision as this would prove, not only to himself, but to those familiar with the incident, he was no longer a man in control of his emotions. He was respected as a King who knew what he wanted, whose decisions had been predetermined without fault. There was no room to cause doubt.

His lunch did not go much differently, but not to the fault of the new cook. The King simply had no appetite. Still, to feel in control, he demanded another new cook without explanation to his staff.

The King was having an unfortunate day, so to brighten his spirits he decided to skip ahead to one of his favorite moments in his daily schedule. He thought, surely it would bring him back to his senses.

He stood atop his castle, overlooking his Kingdom. All he had built with his success, power, and vision. Unfortunately, for him, the day was overcast. While, this occurrence was not uncommon, he wanted to witness all of his glory. He needed to. His eyes failed to give him the satisfaction he sought. Anger burned inside of him again and he cursed the day, hurling insults, and vowed to take command of the sun and sky.

Rather than make his way to his garden for solace, his next routine, he retreated to his bedroom. A daytime slumber had never been an option for the King. It didn't matter. It was not like before. He climbed onto the cold side of his bed, empty of its Queen. A lonely place for what felt like months. He took a deep breath into the pillow and fell asleep.

## King's Wrath
The King awakened as the sun began its decent. The hour to attend his chamber for his nightly entertainment was near. A nagging headache accompanied his half-hearted attempt to force himself out

of bed. He hung his head low as he walked about, still trying to get his wits back from his sleep.

Eventually, he made his way down to his throne, and at just the right moment. All the players came out to greet the King and they immediately began with the night's ceremony.

Unmoved, the King stared off as if in a trance, having vague visions of a past he long abandoned; little moments, flashes of a previous, happy life in which he may have lived long ago. He forgot what it felt like to be happy. The tiny glimpse of this other life was refreshing.

Time passed with other acts trying their hand at amusing the King. Nothing. Greedy Fool, being the best at his position, was well aware of this. He heard the stories of the days earlier, moments of a King short tempered, even sulking, and so he was prepared. He knew if something would be needed to cheer him up it would be to remind him of his power, the control he has maintained over his entire Kingdom.

"Guards!" Greedy Fool shouted, "Bring them in." The King's guards came forward with a family of three.

"My King," Greedy Fool began, "I present to you this family. A family of ungrateful peasants having the audacity of ignoring the tax you have bestowed upon your great Kingdom."

"No, my Lord," the man, head of the family, cried out, "please let me explain!"

"Silence, you filth!" Greedy Fool shouted as he slapped the man across the face. "How dare you speak to the King out of turn? Are you his equal?"

"No, forgive me," the man said shaking his head as he leaned in to huddle with his wife and child. They were terrified.

"Very well, now that they know their place, my Lord, what do you command for their punishment?"

But the King was silent. He stared at the family as if he knew them, or as if he had seen an apparition. Greedy Fool did not know how to respond. He was confused.

"My Lord?" he asked.

"All these years," the King said to himself, "and what do I have to show for it? Perhaps *this* is my curse?"

"My Lord," Greedy Fool tried again, "what is your will? How shall I handle this pestilence within your Kingdom?"

The King was staring at the shivering family when, the young child, a girl, turned toward him. They looked into each other's eyes before she spoke.

"May we go home now?" the child politely asked.

"Silence!" Greedy Fool shouted as he raised his hand to strike the her.

"Stop!" The King roared in such a voice none had ever heard before.

He stood up from his throne and started walking towards Greedy Fool in haste.

"You…"

"My Lord?"

"How dare you make a mockery of me?"

"My King, I assure you…"

"No! I shall have none of it and neither shall you, not anymore!"

The King reached out at Greedy Fool and started attacking him. Greedy Fool was overmatched and pleaded for the King to stop, but being in such a rage, the King could not. Nor could he be reasoned with. He hit him over and over again. No one dared to intervene.

The King screamed one last time at Greedy Fool before exhausting himself. Greedy Fool, in a broken state, laid in agony on the floor. The King turned his attention towards the family, now more frightened than before. He re-gathered himself as best he could and walked cautiously over to them and knelt before the child.

"Forgive me," he said gently, "for I know now what I've done."

The King could no longer control himself. He wept.

"Please," he said as he stood back up. He motioned to his guards to walk over to them.

"They will take you to Greedy Fool's dwelling. There you will find plenty of treasures to last you three lifetimes. Take what your hands can carry and then take more. We will have a carriage outside waiting for you. Go now and thank you for restoring my sight."

The family was in disbelief but expressed their gratitude for his blessings on them. After they left, the King turned his attention back to Greedy Fool.

"And you, you will no longer carry your title here, nor keep what you have earned, kept, or taken for yourself. I have put up with your nature long enough. It has been a poison to me. I do not wish to surround myself with men like you. Not anymore."

Greedy Fool tried to speak, but the pain was too unbearable.

"Guards!" the King commanded, "Take him away at once. Give him little food and provisions. He is to be exiled into the forest. He must never return to this land or he is to face a punishment most cruel."

The guards took Greedy Fool away to the tree line of the forest. They dropped him at an entrance and watched him as he slowly crawled out of their sights and deep into the darkness.

# The Witch

# Chapter 9

## A Child Arrives

The maid servant and her sister made the preparations for the long journey back. It was necessary for them to take a goat to provide for the Princess. The maid servant had no time to waste. The journey was going to take longer with the responsibility of caring for a baby.

To assist, her sister went along as well. With little room left, they attached an additional cart to the back of the wagon to carry the Queen's body.

All the while, the King waited anxiously for the return of his wife, the Queen. He had been in a different state of mind. He no longer desired to keep to his daily schedule, nor did he seek the petty indulgences of entertainment in his chamber. He only ate in small portions, eager to return to his window looking out over any possible sign of his beloved bride.

Back in the forest, the maid servant pushed through the night. She knew she would need to forego much rest. It was up to her sister to watch and tend to the child in the carriage. The Princess slept most of the time, but had moments as if to wake up in a fright.

The maid servant felt pressure on her chest and her eyes had grown weary as she fought the heaviness of sleep.

The forest seemed particularly dark one night, so it was important for her to keep her eyes steady and alert. There were brief moments when her lamp flickered quickly. In those moments, she would see what appeared to be an old woman in black with her eyes veiled over standing just off the side of her riding path. It did not matter how fast they were going. When her lamp flickered, there was the old woman standing, watching as they passed her again and again.

By the fourth day, they finally arrived and exited the forest. The alarm sounded, alerting the King of the arrival. He rushed his way down his castle, through his courtyard and to the entrance to welcome his wife home. He sent word to gather all of the servants and musicians to give her a welcome only fit for a Queen.

Still a stone's throw away, it was obvious something was wrong. The horses seemed too exhausted, sickly even. Once the King arrived, he saw his guards in a hurry to assist the maid servant, too tired to stand on her own, beaten by the trip.

"My Queen! My Queen!" he shouted joyfully as his heart beat faster with every closer step.

Before arriving, he saw a guard with a curious expression on his face upon opening the carriage door. A goat was the first to be carried off. The King was puzzled, but not more so when he heard the cries of a baby. A woman, unknown to him, exited with the infant in her arms.

"What is this? Where is my wife?" he demanded.

"I'm sorry," the maid servant's sister cried out, "during the journey through the forest, your Queen and maid servant faced a horrible danger…"

"Where is she, where is she!?" He demanded once more, but with a look of horror.

"Your Queen," she started, "I'm sorry my lord, but the experience was too much for her heart to handle. She is here, we have wrapped her, and she is now at peace."

Upon hearing her words, the King tore his robe and collapsed face down as he wept near the Queen's body.

"A life of wealth…and no worries…or a life…of struggle?" he said with difficulty. "What have I done? Poor, beautiful woman. I have tortured you for so long, but now it is I that will be tortured, tormented by my actions. My heart aches for the simple times before my sin. Oh, if I could take it back I would, but there is no atonement for me. My place is set, my punishment overdue. I am, now, forever trapped by my misery. But you, my sweet wife, you are no longer of this world. Be free from it, be free from me."

Nothing else mattered to the King after. He blamed no one but himself. He did not bother with any other details about the trip. As far as he was concerned, nothing was of greater value than mourning for his wife. The Kingdom, too, mourned for their Queen and shared stories of her kindness.

## Plan for Revenge

Greedy Fool woke up, somewhere in the vast forest, hurting, angry, and vengeful. He saw his breath floating before him when he felt a sting in his ears. The forest suddenly went cold and the adrenaline of his hate was not sufficient enough to keep him warm.

He lived near the forest his whole life, and knew of the stories about it. He also knew his circumstance would only get worse.

The sounds of hissing surrounded him as snakes slowly slithered their way over. But it didn't matter to him. He was not afraid of the power within the forest. He was too driven with hate to be afraid.

"Where are you?" he shouted. "I have a deal to be made! I know you sense it. When there is a desire as high as mine, you are not far."

And just as quickly as they started, the hissing stopped. The snakes retreated and the temperature ascended.

"Indeed," an old voice echoed near Greedy Fool, "I have never felt such a desire as yours before, such desire."

He could not find the source of the voice, but he didn't need to.

"Then you know I am ready for a deal?"

"Yes, a deal. What is it you seek?"

"I wish to destroy the King, and sit in his place. I want all of his power, all of his glory."

"Of course, no man can resist such a desire, to have the power of a King, what power. But why should I give you what you ask, seek? I will require something in return, yes, something."

"Anything, anything you ask of me."

"That is what I like to hear, but what you seek is not for me to undo, not for me. Perhaps there is something else you desire?"

"No, no. There is nothing else. There is no consolation for me. The King must be destroyed, along with his Queen and their child. He must suffer…"

"What is this you speak of?" the old witch said as she suddenly appeared behind Greedy Fool. "A child?"

"No one knows but me. Not even the King himself. His Queen traveled through this forest to have the child elsewhere in secret."

"You have proven your worth, proven much. It shall be granted, but you must not kill the King. You must instead exile him to me, as he did to you. You will be the cruelest of Kings, so cruel. Many will oppose you and all will fail. Your name will be feared in all the land, it will be feared. How do you wish to do this?"

"Is it now so simple? You said…"

"Do you want me to answer your question, only this question, rather than grant you the revenge you seek?"

"I care not."

"Very well then, very well. How then do you wish to do this?"

With my own army, an army of the dead."

"Done, it is done."

"And what is it you shall have in return of me?"

"Oh, you've done quite enough already, enough."

### Reveal

The King sat on his bed, sobbing, holding the Queen's crown. He had not left his room for days and his cries were heard echoing throughout the castle walls.

"With all my power…all my wealth…I can do what any man in this world can only dream of, but alas, I envy them. This has all been for naught. I sought my own selfish agendas and paid the ultimate price."

"Perhaps it wasn't all bad, not all," an old familiar voice spoke from the darkest corner of the room, "you did indeed achieve all that you asked for, did you not, you did?"

"You," the King replied, "it has indeed been many years past, but the sound of your twisted voice I will never forget. This is all because of you."

"Oh, I heard you quite well as you said before. You are to blame, you are. I am but a humble servant giving a man his desire to become more than simply a man, I gave."

The King was still unable to see the witch.

"It was all by your trickery, you deceived me."

"No!" she shouted back, "I gave you all you asked. Nothing more, nothing less. It is you that has deceived, and I am here to collect what is rightfully mine, thus, ending our little arrangement, it ends."

"I don't understand you. Your speech is bad enough and now you insist on speaking in riddles?"

"When I first met you, you were a young naive little man with nothing but a new little bride. You had nothing, but you wanted much, wanting. You were desperate to keep what little land you had with your wife. You needed to save her, did you not? So desperate to make a deal with me? A deal that would make you King, a strong and powerful King, so strong. Never to lose in battle, your name alone could rule your Kingdom, all alone. To have a life of wealth and without any more worries, no more. You wanted to change the world, you have. And it was in this deal we made the price for such a gift to be your firstborn child, the first. But by breaking your promise, I can now break mine, broken."

"I've tried to forget. I've tried and succeeded, if only for a time, there was never a deal made. My happiness was only short lived. I could not look at my wife without the sting of guilt pitted in my stomach, knowing she was oblivious, knowing she didn't understand why I was so difficult. She wanted children but I made sure we never had to lose one of them to you. In my pride, I had forgotten why I didn't want children and soon despised the idea. But I never had a child, so if you are here for a collection, you can take me. I have nothing more to gain or live for in this life."

"I did not think I would have ever met a man with more desire than you, so much desire. That is, until I met the man you refer to as Greedy Fool, so greedy."
The King looked fearfully in the direction of her voice.

"I do not believe him to be a man as compromising in his decisions as you have proven to be. As we speak, he is amassing an army of the dead to steal your title as King and rule the very world you have created, your world."

"Even with an army of the dead, none can defeat me, as part of our arrangement. You said it yourself, 'by name alone you will rule this Kingdom.'"

"Have you not listened to a word I have spoken? I have. You have kept from me this little child, you kept. And now, she is rightfully mine, my right."

"What is this you speak of? Show yourself!" The witch stepped forward, out of the shadows, holding the sleeping baby, Princess Elise.

"What child is this?" the King asked.

"Why King, it is yours," she said with delight, "and now it is mine, now."

"I have no children."

"When Greedy Fool came to me, he told me something even you, the all-powerful King, did not know of, he told me. Perhaps, had you not showed such contempt towards your Queen, you would have seen what was in front of you the whole time, such contempt. She was with child. I know this, I know now. Even in her old age, and it killed her. The child she so desperately wanted, even if it took her life, dead."

"No, this cannot be true, you demon!"

"I was drawn to her carriage on her journey back. I could sense my prize, mine."

The King fell to his knees and begged.

"Please, if this is true, take my Kingdom, all that I have is yours. Let me have my child."

"I don't need your possessions, no need. All of the men I have made my deals with all want the same things and I always get from them what I want, I get from them."

She gave a shrieking laugh, stepped back into the dark and vanished.

Immediately after, the King could hear the shouts of his men and the sounds of battle. Without hesitation, the King took up arms and went out to the front lines. All he could think about was surviving. The child he had never known was his only concern. His Kingdom, his riches, his power, none of it had mattered anymore. He needed to find the witch and rescue his daughter.

# Princess Elise

# Eight Years

Eight years passed since the King first woke up on the cold soil deep within the dark forest. His castle was overrun by Greedy Fool's army of the dead quickly and, seemingly, with little effort.

Greedy Fool greeted his dark Kingdom everyday atop the castle. He enjoyed the view of his wealth and inheritance. Still, it was more enjoyable watching his army instill fear into his subjects. It reminded him of his power and his control.

All items and statues built for and by his predecessor were torn down. Larger, gold statues of the new king were put in their place. The King's throne and crown now belonged to Greedy Fool.

"While I take joy in my inheritance as a Fool, a Fool I am no longer. Although, I must say, 'Greedy' suits me just fine. And all the lands will forever know the name of King Greedy!"

The witch took great physical care of Princess Elise to ensure her body was strong. She had taken care of her body but cared not for her mind. As the child grew, the witch kept her as a prisoner in a dark room. She made no secret to the child she was orphaned and held for a later purpose. She educated her enough to understand what it meant to be unloved.

Being alone, the Princess found comfort by experimenting with the sounds of her voice. She first took to humming, imitating birds of the forest, which eventually led to singing. However, the witch did not take too kindly to it. Using her power in anger, she uttered, "No more words, none." Immediately; the mouth of the Princess was sewn shut, only to unravel when it was time for her to eat.

Princess Elise was alone and scared. She had never known happiness nor had she ever seen a loving smile. And yet, nothing was more frightening to her than the first moment she started hearing a voice.

During the eight years, the King endured much. He was driven mad. His life was in constant danger, trapped within the vast and mystical forest. He faced unimaginable creatures, was forced to withstand temperatures of extreme heat and cold, and forced to witness horrific visions of his dead wife. The forest used her image to torture him in the moments he wanted to think of her. Often times, he saw her dead corpse roaming aimlessly while her body slowly deteriorated. On occasion, she held her severed head as it cried hysterically.

His quest to rescue his daughter was his last source of strength, but the forest took its toll on him. He questioned his sanity many times, even his purpose to find the witch. After eight years of surviving, of searching, he grew tired and was full of despair. He considered taking his own life, or simply allowing the evils in the forest to swallow him up.

Regardless, his body was weak, and he laid down for what he expected to be his final rest. He cried out one last time in agony,

"There is no hope! There is no hope!"

Exhausted, he fell asleep.

Out of the woods, a rabbit raced to his side. It sat by him and waited. It waited for him to wake up so it could show him the way to Hope.

# Hope

# Chapter 10

## Humble Home

Out in the country side, far away from the king's castle was a man named Eli, tending to his sheep. He did not have many. His home was small, nothing to be admired. Still, he was happy. What little livestock he owned belonged to him and his new bride, Sarai. Not far from them lived her parents with their own small home and livestock.

Eli and Sarai had known each other since they were children. They lived through the best and worst of times together.

Eli lost both of his parents early in life due to a great war. They were killed in their home as Eli and Sarai hid together in a wine press. So, Sarai's parents took him in when he had no one else, and loved him as a son.

Not long after, a plague struck the land and claimed the lives of many, including all of Sarai's siblings. Still, through all the death and darkness they always had each other. They were inseparable.

Sarai's parents knew they had a special relationship and looked forward to the day of their daughter's marriage to Eli. This was their silver lining, their last chance for hope, their last source of strength to carry them on for the rest of their days.

Eli and Sarai lived a simple life and they planned for many children, many whose names were already decided.

When Eli finished tending to his sheep, he started to prep his ox to plow. This was when a letter carrier arrived.

"Good day, sir," Eli greeted.

Without hesitation, the man gave his message.

"By order of our new king, all of your cattle shall be given over for his royal army," he said as he handed him the decree.

"But, sir, I have only two. I need…"

"What you need, *sir* is to do right by your king. Need I remind you that you are only here on this land to tend to it? It is only allowable because he pities men such as yourself and, thus, allows your stay. This land belongs to him. You should be grateful, boy."

Eli had no choice in the matter. The following morning his ox and cow were taken by two of the king's royal guards. As the guards were loading the cattle, they both took notice of Sarai's beauty.

Eli watched helplessly, powerless alongside Sarai as they took the cattle away.

"We'll get through this one," she said, "we are not strangers to dire situations. We'll survive. We always do."

"But what kind of husband am I? We have been married but two months and already we have less than what we started with."

"Why, my husband, who said we have less?" Sarai then held him close, "Not long from now we will have one more mouth to feed, and I will give up two cattle for a child any day," she said with a smile.

Upon hearing this, Eli was overjoyed. This was the first time he heard she was with child.

Their momentary troubles seemed bleak, but their future was exciting, and it could not come any sooner for them. Their lives were still ahead of them and having a child was only the beginning.

"We'll make it work," he said, "as long as we have each other, we'll always make it work."

That same night, Eli went to bed with a great sense of urgency. He knew the moment he closed his eyes he would wake up one day closer to seeing their child born. It would be the happiest day of their lives.

## Waking Up

The King of old, now a widower and father of Princess Elise, was awakened by a tickling sensation on his face. It had been eight years of struggle and torment. His will to fight, driven by his guilt, was gone. The wicked forest swallowed his spirit. He was a living lost soul, similar to the apparitions wandering about, and he was ready to join them in death.

His eyes were still heavy, exhausted. He was a broken man, but he was also surprised. He felt as though death was certain for him, yet, there he lay, still in the terrible forest, still alive.

He felt the sensation again on his face.

"Time to wake up, mighty King," a voice spoke.

The King was able to shake his head and focus his eyes on to the trees surrounding him. Still, he could see no person there, only a rabbit by his head.

"Who said that?" the King asked as he surveyed the area.

"I did," the rabbit responded just as their eyes met. Although weak, the King had enough energy to distance himself from the rabbit out of fear.

"What are you? Am I dead? Did the witch send you to torment me some more? Are you here to finish me off?"

"No, your majesty, I am a messenger of Hope, but I must say, you do look as good as dead. I even thought you might have been if only for a moment," the rabbit replied.

The King could not gather his wits.

"This is what I have been reduced to," he said to himself, "I've gone mad. A sickness in my mind. I am now both victim and tormentor."

"Your majesty, I assure you..."

"And yet it continues to speak, making a mockery of me. Be gone, rabbit! Can I not die in peace?"

The King threw a stone at the rabbit. It scurried off and was soon out of sight.

"At last, my time has come to..."

"Your majesty, if I may..." the rabbit interrupted him from behind, once again, giving him a fright.

"Ah! Instrument of torture, leave me be!" the King cried out, now rocking, clasping his head, and keeping his eyes shut tight.

"Now, now…there is no need for name calling. As I said before, I am a messenger of Hope. I am here to help you."

"Hope?" the King replied, "There is no Hope."

"There is always Hope. Unfortunately for you, you gave up long before your stay in this forest. Am I wrong in what I say?"

The King's mind was too preoccupied to carry a conversation. It was at a fragile state having endured endless torment. He had a break down for some time and, therefore, could not comprehend what the rabbit was trying to tell him.

"The witch," the King said as if he had a new idea, "she has kept me alive with these awful berries falling from the trees. I confuse them with insects. It doesn't matter. They taste the same. But rabbit! Ah, yes! I have not tasted rabbit for some time. Oh, how I've longed for a feast such as this!"

The King quickly looked around for a large stick with which to kill the rabbit. He settled for a hanging branch along the trunk of a tree. However, as he reached for it, the rabbit struck the back of the King's head into the tree, knocking him out.

"Tomorrow will be a better day," the rabbit said.

## Blue Moon

Locked away in her dark room, Princess Elise would stare up through a window eight feet high, looking to catch more of the world outside. She would stand and stare, looking up, for many hours at a time. The window allowed the sunlight to shine through to one single spot in the room. This is where she stood, out of the darkness.

However, her favorite time of day was night because only then could she see the stars. She studied their movements helping her keep track of her days and the changing seasons. She grew very accustomed to learning the intricacies of the night sky within the confines of the window frame. More than anything else, she loved the sight of the moon.

On this particular night, she had the perfect vantage point to witness it in full. It was a grand sight for her, as if she was its only audience. The moon was vast, blue, and it shined through her window, lighting up an otherwise dark room. It gave her a sense of much needed peace.

"Let your light shine, blue moon," she would think to herself.

During her eight years under the care of the witch, the Princess was on a very strict diet to ensure she retained a healthy body. She ate three meals a day. The portions were not too much or too little, always the right amount and never with any traces of fat.

For exercise, the witch permitted the Princess time outside in a contained area. This was when she could see the animals of the forest. They were all beautiful to her. She imagined they were part of a larger family, loved and happy, unlike her.

She was secluded and inexperienced in life, but Princess Elise had a vivid imagination, which was mostly explored through her dreams. Unfortunately, these were not always welcome or pleasant. She had many recurring dreams about trying to escape her captivity, but they were frightening to her. They were dark, scary, and never ended well.

Even in her dreams she was trapped. She could never escape because she didn't believe she could. Above all, she didn't think she had a reason to. She lived in the only reality she knew to exist, without having a sense of purpose. She even had small sentiments for the witch. She was, after all, the only mother she had, for better or worse. The witch successfully convinced her she was alone, unloved by her parents, orphaned and unwanted by anyone else.

There was another recurring dream she would have. Not like the others and not nearly as often. It would come once, the same time each year; the Princess recognized this through the alignment of the stars.

She never understood it, but in her dream, she would see momentary pictures, quick flashes of a woman's face. The face was never clear enough to see, rather, it was cloudy, but the face was always close and always bearing a smile, something she had only seen in this dream. The woman's mouth would then move as if she was saying something to the Princess, but the words remained incoherent; sounds going in and out, jumbled, and without clarity.

Nothing compared to the moment she would awake from this particular dream. It was a stronger sensation than the one given by the sight of the moon. She didn't know what to call the feeling, but it felt good.

King Greedy

# Chapter 11

**Firstborn**

Within the eight years of his rule, King Greedy was vile and ruthless; showing no remorse or pity. Spread throughout all the lands were small platoons of King Greedy's army of the dead. They were in place to enforce his rule and ready to extinguish any attempts of rebellion against him.

During his first year in power, daring men managed to create a sizable army to challenge King Greedy. They consisted of mighty warriors, men willing to risk their very lives if it meant saving the ones they loved.

They were careful and concise with their plans. Any other, natural, army of men would have fallen to their attack. However, their enemies were not ordinary, so it was all in vain. Their plans were man-made using only their worldly wisdom as if they were fighting other men. The dead army, created with dark magic by the witch, was capable of performing supernatural feats.

One soldier from the dead army could easily put to the sword thirty men in little time. Although the Dead, as they were simply called, started out only as one hundred, their strength was in their immortality and resurrection. They could not die a second time. Even if maimed, this would merely slow them down. In time, they would reattach their severed parts to their rotted corpses.

Another sign of being a product of darkness was the ability to give birth to death: any man killed by one of them was reborn into their ranks. They quickly grew in number.

All the while, King Greedy enjoyed the slaughter of battle from the top of his castle. Always with one dead soldier standing guard at his side, he would call out orders to it and it was as if he were speaking to all of them.

"Spare one hundred," he commanded, "and gather them. I wish to send a message."

After the fight, King Greedy approached the defeated soldiers.

"I've been your king but for a few months. My wish was only to rule and enjoy the spoils that are rightfully mine. And yet, you have already forced my hand. Well, I promise you this; I will not spare the rod. I, your king, must punish you, my pathetic peasants. Most of you may be allowed to live simply so you may retreat like a wounded dog back to your homes to tell anyone with ears…that all of your firstborns will be put to death. This is a promise to you and your children, and all those far off. I want you to remember this day!"

Upon hearing this, the men fell face down, crying out to the king. They begged for forgiveness, pleaded for mercy, and even offered their own lives in place of the children. King Greedy relished hearing their voices as they trembled with fear.

Immediately, without further warning, thirty of the one hundred men were struck down by the Dead for they themselves were firstborns. The king made good on his promise.

From then on, the army of the dead dispersed throughout the lands proclaiming the king's promise via their slaughter; killing firstborns, young and old alike. There was no value in trying to escape or hide from this fate. By obeying the word of their king, the Dead had instinctive knowledge as to who were firstborns and where to find them.

To commemorate the day, a decree was written, demanding a firstborn child in each divided land to be sacrificed in the king's honor every year. Events such as this were only the beginning of the pains the land would suffer during his dark reign.

By the end of eight years, good land for farming had become scarce. The Kingdom was a wasteland. Markets were overrun by beggars and the sick. Men, women, and children were desperate enough to openly attempt to steal, even kill, if it meant providing for their families. There were no laws to be upheld only to live by their natural instincts for survival. They were left to fend for themselves; some through mercy and compassion, others through selfish and calloused desperation. Without a leader to guide them, it was difficult to find a way to live together.

Often times, King Greedy would survey the land to see the people throw themselves at his feet to beg. If he was amused enough by their suffering he would give small portions of food.

The land was restless, yet, King Greedy was at peace. His personal livestock numbered well above tens of thousands, while his private lands produced the best fruits and vegetables. His servants were numerous so as to keep up with the day to day chores around his castle as well as to tend to the livestock and farming.

Being a servant to the king was both a blessing and a curse. It was a blessing because they were able to survive and were given just enough to care for their immediate families. However, not only did they need to be mindful of King Greedy's wrath, but they were not protected from outside threats. If they strayed too far from the castle's doors or even outside the lines of his private lands, they were attacked, beaten, and killed, leaving an opening for the king's service. The murderers would then take the place of their victims and none would be the wiser, except for their families.

## Path

Since the beginning of King Greedy's rule, the maid servant had been stricken with guilt. She was unable to fulfill the promise she made to her Queen; to look after the Princess and to raise her as her own.

On many sleepless nights, she forced herself to relive the moments before Princess Elise was taken from her care. There was a void in this memory. She could only remember trying to hide the baby from the battle and then waking up alone on the floor. Since then, she assumed the child to be dead.

During the chaos of the takeover, her sister managed to escape. She was hesitant to leave but the maid servant was too hysterical to reason with; she was running all over the castle looking for the Princess. Men were slain in front of her, but she could not bother her mind with anything other than finding the baby.

For the past eight years, she reluctantly served King Greedy. He was familiar with many of the servants and wished to keep those he knew to serve exceptionally well. She had no choice in the matter, either serve the king or face death.

One night, while she stared off at the moon and stars from her window, she thought about the Princess and what she might look like after eight years.

"She would be beautiful, just like her mother," said a voice coming from behind her.

The maid servant gasped and jumped forward out of fear. She expected to see an intruder in her home, someone desperate to take her place as a servant. There was no one to be found.

"Who is there?" She alarmingly muttered, "Who said that?"

"Be not afraid ma'am," the voice said. Looking down, she noticed a small mouse on the floor staring directly at her.

"There is no need to worry," the mouse spoke again.

"You are a messenger of Hope?" she asked without fear in her voice, but frustration.

"It is as you say."

"Then give him a message for me. Tell him to leave me alone and do what would be best for the Kingdom and go away. You are no better than a bedtime story giving children false promises. You may know how to conjure talking creatures, but you are just as useless as my imagination!"

"Are you finished?" the mouse asked.

"No! Where were you? Why did you not rescue the Princess? Now she is lost forever. The Kingdom is lost too. It's been eight years and you are *now* showing up?"

"Perhaps I *should* leave because my timetable does not suit you. Do not mistake absence for lack of compassion. Instead of asking where I have been, ask yourself where *you* have been."

"I have been here, waiting for you."

"Yes, you have been here, but if you had really sought me, you would have found me. Instead, you stand there in your self-pity blaming me when you have done nothing to seek out the truth."

"And what is the truth?"

"The Princess is alive."

The maid servant was taken aback by the news.

"And yet, you still doubt?" the mouse continued, "Stop doubting and believe!" he pleaded with her.

"What must I do to help her? Where is she? Where has she been?"

"The witch of the forest has been holding her captive. If you wish to save her, you mustn't stay here any longer. You need to go into the forest. There will be further instructions when you are there, but you must go now!"

The maid servant, along with the mouse, snuck out of the living quarters and made their way to the familiar entrance of the safe path through the forest. Before she could step forward, she hesitated when she realized she did not have any of the necessary counter measures against the magic of the forest.

"Must I push you in?" asked the mouse.

"You don't understand, these remedies have been passed down many generations. Without them…"

"Without them, your faith is stronger. Someone long ago decided their faith wasn't enough and so they took it upon themselves to add superstitions, contrary to what was already long established."

"And what was that?"

"This path through darkness was and has always been the creation of Hope. You do not have to make up your own rules. Do not be misled, not even by your own experience. It is a safe path to take."

"Very well," she replied.

Still, she felt uneasy stepping into the forest alone. After treading lightly passed the tree line, she turned to thank the mouse, but he was gone.

Once again, she turned to the way leading into the forest. There was no going back for her. She needed to throw off her fear and replace it with every bit of courage she had. Having found her purpose, she was ready to walk the path.

### Inside the Monster

Abaddon wandered the forest aimlessly, without human guidance or reason. It walked about only to satisfy its appetite. When the creature had more than its fill, it would find its way to the top of a tree for a deep sleep. It was in these moments the mind of the Butcher feared the most. The more exhausted the creature was, the deeper the sleep would be, and the more vivid his dreams were.

Countless times, he was forced to relive the horror of what he had become. In those dreams, he would wake up as the Butcher in his bed along with his wife. Their two children would soon run into his bedroom to greet him with laughter and love, celebrating the life they lived.

His day would be a typical one in the former life of the Butcher. He would go to work, even settle matters and disputes throughout the day for the townspeople.

At night, they would all celebrate the town's prosperity with a festival; music, dancing, and other merriment to carry the night away.

Every one of these dreams would take a turn for the worse. Always, it would begin with the Butcher becoming catatonic, unable to move. He would then be forced to watch what unfolded. Out of the darkness, his other half, Abaddon, would charge forward, striking with every ounce of ferocity it had.

The Butcher would scream out to his family to run. He would beg for Abaddon to leave them alone. It would always kill them. The outcome was set. Although he never gets to hold them as they lay dying, their blood would always appear on his hands.

After its slumber, the Butcher would always awaken to Abaddon tearing through the flesh of some poor creature. Eating…always eating.

# Chapter 12

## An Old Woman's Offering

Even without cattle, Eli and Sarai were making the most of what they had. They didn't give up believing they could finally live out their dreams for a happy life.

Eli was tending to his sheep when he noticed someone standing at the far end of his land facing towards him. At first, he thought little of it, but the person never moved, only stood and stared. So, he made his way over to see who it was.

Although she was far off, he could tell it was an old woman, even though her face was partially concealed.

"Can I help you?" he shouted as he closed the distance.

She said not a word. She waited.

After he arrived he asked again, "Can I help you? Are you looking for someone?"

"Yes, looking, yes," she said strangely and with an odd voice, "Who, indeed, you in fact…yes, you."

"Do I know you? My name is…"

"Eli, yes, but you know me not. Not yet."

"And how, may I ask, do you know me?"

"I sensed a desire in you. It was small and quick, but enough to get my attention, enough."

"A desire?"

"You wish to be rid of your current unpleasantries, rid them all. Have comfort. Raise a family with more on your plates, more mouths to feed."

"It wouldn't be difficult to assume this, my home and possessions aren't much to look at, but I'm sorry, you are mistaken. I am content with what I have and dare not change it. I wouldn't want to risk happiness for my family."

"Be that as it may, I trust my senses, I trust. There is something more you seek, perhaps not at this moment, not this, but you will come back around to it."

Eli was losing his patience with her.

"Although, you are simply near my land, know you are not welcome on it. I must be going."

"Before you go," she said, stopping him from turning around, "here is what I am offering."

She extended her hand towards him revealing a fig in her palm.

"What is this?" he asked.

"Take this, you must both eat from it, both of you, and you will have life to the full, have your fill."

"That is nonsense!"

Eli turned once more and looked towards his home. He could see there was some commotion. Fear struck him immediately and he started to run. The closer he got, the more it was clear what was happening.

There was a struggle. He screamed out. There was nothing he could do, but scream out. He saw his in-laws struck down as they battled two men, one holding Sarai. He could hear her screaming, screaming out for him.

Before his arrival, they threw her on one of the horses. He recognized the men. They were soldiers in the king's army, the same ones from before. Having already taken his cattle, they returned for Sarai.

He was too late. They were gone. The horror unfolded before him and he could do nothing about it.

He noticed his father in-law struggling, dying before him. In his last breaths, he spoke to Eli.

"They said…she belongs to the king now. Don't…don't let her go. Whatever you do…don't let her go."

His father in-law died there in his arms. He did not have any horses, but he knew the longer he did nothing the more danger Sarai faced.

"Yes, my senses are right, my senses," the old woman spoke as she was now, suddenly, standing behind Eli.

He was too preoccupied in thought to give a response to the old woman.

"If it is a horse you seek," she began, "a fast horse, I have plenty."

"Yes! Please!" She now had Eli's attention, "I beg you. Lend me a horse so I may rescue my wife."

"The horse will be here shortly, on my call, here. But first, your desire is great. So much pain before…this life, yours, hers. And now? Yes, now it is still. Perhaps there is more for you, more? I have helped many, such as you."

"Thank you for your kindness. For now, I simply require a horse."

"Yes, require, yet, you still desire more. Perhaps you save your wife from the soldiers or the king, but it will not end there, will not. There will be more, more struggle and pain."

"What are you suggesting?"

"A trade."

"What is it you seek? I will give you all I have for your horse."

"Boy, have you not heard me? There is more which I can offer, more than a horse. I offer your desire. To live a life of wealth and no worries, or a life of struggle?"

"That is impossible. Please, I just need your horse."

Through his desperation, Eli considered briefly killing the old woman if just to take her horse, should it arrive.

"Yes, such desire," she started, now with excitement in her voice, "but you cannot kill me not by your hands, cannot."

The old woman then gave a shrieking laugh. In a matter of seconds, the sky was overcast. It drew black. The old woman rose in the air, carried by some invisible force. Eli fell to his knees trembling.

"What are you?" he asked.

"What matters is what I can do for you, matters. You may have doubted before, but now you have seen my power."

"Yes, I see."

"Without my help, you can make it to the castle in three days' time, exhausted, little fight left. You may be too late, too weak. However, if you want to save her, your wife, tonight, it is a heavy price. Much to consider."

"Whatever it takes! With all my heart, if you can provide what you say, I will give you whatever you ask." The old woman smiled and enjoyed her moment.

"Take this," she said, handing him a fig, "both of you must share a bite, share. It will make you strong for your journey, protect you. You will surely not die. It will be your food for your travel, no hunger. And you *must* have her take a bite, she must. All the land will be yours, all. You must take it, you will be King and your name alone will rule, you."

Eli didn't hesitate any longer. He took a bite and he immediately felt rejuvenated, refreshed. The horse finally arrived and he mounted it, riding off as fast as the horse was capable, ready to give his life to save the

woman he loved.

# Chapter 13

**Safe Place**

Back in the forest, the King, once again, was surprised to open his eyes. He was able to look around, but he couldn't move. He was tied to a tree.

"Am I not dead yet?" he started, "Oh…perhaps one of my enemies of old will happen by and release me from my misery!"

Out of the corner of his eye, he saw movement. He looked over, but could not catch a glimpse of who or what was moving about.

"Hello?" he asked suspiciously.

There was no answer, only what he heard to be feet running back and forth behind him.

"Are you such a coward you cannot face a dying man tied to a tree?" he shouted out.

Then he heard the sound of their laughter just before they ran within inches passed him. He saw two children, both very young. One wore a helmet much too large for his head. They did not take any notice of the King there tied to the tree. They just played.

"Children!" he called out, "This is not a safe place to play. You should go home now and never return!" Again, they paid no attention to him. There was no reply, no acknowledgment of his existence.

"Perhaps this is another vision?" he asked himself, "So they are to suffer before me, to remind me of my sin." The King had no choice but to sit and watch.

He anticipated a horrible fate for them. He imagined their demise coming from a creature attacking from the forest, or they would simply hurt themselves, severely, by accident. He waited. With every small sound, whether the wind or an animal passing through, he was on high alert. Yet, nothing happened.

They continued to play carefree with danger nowhere to be found. This went on long enough for the King to forget about his momentary troubles. Something changed in him. He stared as though he were in a trance, taken to another place by their innocence and joy. Soon, he found himself laughing along with them. He could not remember the last time he laughed with such happiness and peace.

Suddenly, without warning, they both looked up over passed the King's head, as if someone was calling them. They smiled, ear to ear, and started making their way back from where they had come. The older of the two picked up his pace and ran passed the King, while the younger, the one wearing the helmet, walked slowly. The child removed the large helmet from his head and held it in his hand as if it were fragile. When he was close to the King, he placed the helmet at his feet. He smiled directly at him just before running off to catch up to the older child.

"What is this?" he thought to himself, "Am I dead? Has this curse finally been lifted? Could this be…Hope?" Immediately, the ropes loosened and the King was able to remove the restraints, freeing himself.

He stood up with the helmet in his hands. Nobody was in sight. All was quiet.

"Do you believe now?" said a familiar voice beside him, breaking the silence.
The King turned toward the voice. Looking down, he saw the rabbit from before.

"It is you again," said the King, "how is it possible my troubles have escaped me?"

"Do not be mistaken, those troubles are still here and you will still need to face them."

"How can I? I am but a shell of a man, unworthy of being a slave."

"Consider the children for a moment: innocent, jovial, born trusting the world. The mind of a child can be very fragile, easily manipulated, and impressionable. Still, they all begin the same. It is just a matter of time before they are exposed to darkness, to the corruption in this world they are born into. Their futures are never certain, for when a child is born, possibilities are endless. With every birth, they bring light to the world, giving life to Hope."

"How does this help me?"

"Look to the children if you want to overcome the darkness. You need to renew your mind, reawaken it. It has become depraved, swallowed up by fear and regret.

You must believe and not doubt. You have been lost for some time, long before you were sentenced here, and you did it to yourself, you gave up."

"I can barely remember anything before this. It all seemed like a dream. I don't know what drives me anymore."

"Your daughter awaits you. While her mind is being poisoned with doubt, there still remains a glimmer of Hope left in her."

"What father am I? I am no father. I gave up that right long ago."

"It is time for you to come back to your senses!" shouted the rabbit.

This surprised the King.

"Yes," the rabbit continued, "at this particular moment you are a coward, undeserving because of your selfishness. Unfortunately, this doesn't change the circumstances for your daughter. She is not any less your own simply because you wish to look away. You once fought for someone you loved. You must do it again. You must not give up!"

The King considered what he just heard and thought about a future he once dreamed of with his Queen. He could see her face clearly in his thoughts. How he longed to hold her. It was in this moment he saw her apparition peer out from behind a tree ahead of him. He dropped to his knees and began to cry out to her.

"Please! I cannot bare the sight of her death before me. Not again!"

The King worried the forest would continue its torment over him by showing his Queen continually die horrible deaths. The light in the forest started to dim and a heavy fog materialized.

"You must not give up on Hope or it will defeat you!" the rabbit shouted to the King, "The forest is tempting you. It wants you to fail."

"How? How can I overcome this?" The air turned cold and leaves spun around by a strong gust of wind.

"Resist it!" again, the rabbit shouted, "You must deny your fears and your doubt."

The King looked to the helmet and instinctively put it on his head. The ghostly image of the Queen glided towards him. When she was within arm's reach, the King had become completely immersed in the fog. It was cold and wet, yet he felt a burning sensation. He thought the fog brought him to his death.

He could not see anything else around him except the face of the Queen, staring into his eyes. However, this was not like before. He wasn't scared. She was different.

Her face was sweet, a beautiful sight. He was, again, reminded of a life they had once dreamed together. He could see his life unfold as he looked into her eyes. They took him back to the day of her death. He could see himself holding her lifeless body. The moment was especially painful because it was too late for him to show her he could still be the man she married.

"It's not too late," she whispered to him. Almost as quickly as the moment arrived, it ended. The fog faded, the light returned to the forest, and the Queen dissipated into the air. The King, in vain, tried to touch her, but she was gone.

"What must I do?" he asked the rabbit.

"Fight! You can expect a war coming to you. Not long from now, the witch will likely sense your renewed strength and set her dark magic against you."

"How can I face her?"

The rabbit smiled before answering:

"With Hope, of course."

# Chapter 14

**Sparrow**

The next morning, the witch entered Princess Elise's room with the same greeting:

"Wake up, orphan, wake. Even those unloved must eat."

The witch placed the food on a small table in the room. She would then wave her hand in front of Elise, untying the stitches and freeing her mouth.

"You must get your fill, you must. Tomorrow is the beginning, the end. Your purpose has required much patience, much from me. Still, better to be patient than take a city, much better."

"Will I get to go outside?" the Princess asked just before she started to eat her food.

"Yes, of course. That is where you will be, as I."

Elise ate her food in haste, she was eager to ask a question. She could not simply ask after having started on her meal. The witch was very strict about making sure she ate all of the food given to her. So much so, she waited in the room for her to finish.

"What is my purpose? You have not told me. I know I will die soon, but for what?" she asked immediately after taking her last bite.

"To destroy Hope," the witch said with an evil grin. "Even if only for a little while, it will be enough, gone."

"Who is Hope, your enemy?"

"He is all that stands in my way, all, keeping me confined to my trees. I have little influence, power outside. Without Hope, I can walk freely, do as I please, freely. Then I can bring darkness in all the land."

"Why must you hate so?" the Princess asked with such displeasure.

"It is what I am!" the witch shouted as she waved her hand once again to reseal Elise's mouth. She left her alone in her dark room.

"Why must it be me?" the Princess thought to herself, "If only death would come sooner."
She wept.

"There is no need to cry child," an unfamiliar voice said.

Elise looked around her room frightened. She did not know where the voice came from. Since she could not speak, she could not call out to the stranger.

"I can hear your thoughts, talk to me," the voice encouraged.

The Princess suddenly became terrified. She could not see anyone speaking, so she assumed it was coming from her mind.

"No more words, none!" she attempted to scream out.

She clasped her head with both of her hands, afraid to lose command of her thoughts. They were all she had control over, all she had to bring her peace.

"I assure you, child, I am merely here to help you."

"You mustn't be in my head. It is all I have!"

"And it will continue to be yours, but you have much more than you realize."

"Please, I beg you. This is my life and it will come soon to an end. I need my mind."

"Child, listen closely. You will not bring about the death of Hope; rather, you will bring him to life for the rest of the world. Now please, look up toward your window."

The Princess did. She saw a sparrow perched on the open frame.

"You are not from my mind?" she asked cautiously.

"No, child," he simply replied.

"What a wonderful looking creature you are. What are you?"

"The creature you see before you is known as a sparrow. There are many creatures like myself, messengers of Hope. We carry his good news and help those who seek him or are in need of him."

"So, you are here to help me?"

"I am here to prepare you. I cannot simply help you escape, the witch will know. She is powerful here.

You may need to suffer a little more, but only for a short while until your father, the King, comes."

The news surprised her. This was the first time she heard her father was still alive. The witch told her stories about her parents, leading her to believe they had given her up, leaving her unloved and unwanted. She was also told they died horrible deaths, killing one another.

"My father is alive? Why would he come for me? He does not love me. He let me come here. He gave me to hurt, to die," she told him as her eyes began to tear once more.

"The witch has tried to poison your mind. She took you from him. Since that day, your father has been in this terrible forest looking for you, surviving unimaginable horrors."

"But the witch said…"

"She is a liar, the mother of all lies. *Your* mother, the Queen, bore you and died for you out of love. She did not know what your future held, but she had Hope. And it is out of love your father will fight for you, even in the face of death. He is ready to save you because he has Hope, and you now have him too."

### Always a Fool

During one of his favorite times of the day, King Greedy stood atop his castle to stare out at all he ruled. There were numerous monuments built in his honor. The land was full of despair, but he was incapable of having empathy. Instead, he considered how many more monuments he needed built throughout the lands. For him, there could never be enough.

It was in this moment he noticed a man, standing and staring up towards him. The man never moved. A fight broke out between two other men less than ten feet from where he stood and, yet, he remained still, standing and staring.

"How curious," King Greedy thought to himself. "Bring him up," he told the dead soldier by his side.

The king was sitting on his throne when the man was brought in to see him. He looked broken, beat down. His hair was wild. His clothing was poorly put together. His eyes were wide, staring off, never making eye contact. He was malnourished, frail, and sickly. As he stood before King Greedy, he mumbled silently to himself.

"Well now," started the king, "you are in the presence of your lord, by all means, speak up man and tell me what it is you seek."

The man did not flinch. He stared about, eyes fixing on different objects in the enormous room, still mumbling.

"Have you forgotten how to speak?" the king asked with a laugh, amused by the man's suffering.

"Speak?" the man suddenly blurted, starting to come to his senses. He finally made eye contact with the king before saying it again, "Speak…speak for those unable to speak for themselves. My family…gone. Murdered. Unjustly. Without pity. You have taken their voice. The sound of their laughter…gone forever. For what? So a Fool can feel important? Not a man, never a man, always a Fool! Certainly, not any king of mine!"

"Strike him!" King Greedy shouted in anger. One of the dead soldiers hit the man on the back of the head, knocking him face first to the floor. King Greedy stood from his throne, sword in hand, and walked to the man as he lay down trying to regain his wits.

"A Fool…always a Fool," the man struggled to say.

"A king," he responded coldly.

"No…you only have power as long as the witch allows it. Someone will go to her, someone such as you, ready to make a deal for a black heart. We are all desperate enough. It is only a matter of time."

The man suddenly laughed hysterically as he continued to mock the king, "A Fool, always a Fool, always a Fool…"

King Greedy pierced the man's heart with his sword. He dropped it and wandered over to his balcony facing the forest. He stared at the trees and realized the man was right.

## Into the Water

The maid servant walked for hours on the path of Hope. No messengers visited her and there were no signs for instruction. Still, the path was clear, with enough light to guide her.

From her vantage point, she could see the dark creatures of the forest moving about within the trees, roaming, as if looking for something to hunt. Every once in a while, a crow would fly onto the path in an attempt to frighten her off of it, but she knew how important it was to stay on. Should she falter off course, it could lead to her death.

Although she had taken this route before, it looked different. Something changed. There was a winding in the road ahead. This was unexpected and not as before. It struck her as odd. She wanted to question why she had never seen this before, but she convinced herself it was part of what Hope wanted for her. She didn't understand, but she needed to trust.

After walking the curve, she noticed a small pond cutting off the way. In order to get to the other side, and stay on the path, she needed to swim through.

The water was warm to the touch. Without question, she jumped in, eager to move forward.

She was completely immersed. This was unlike any other time she had gone for a swim. This was more than getting wet. Underneath the water, she saw a vision of herself struggling, drowning, pulled down by unseen forces, taken deeper and deeper into the abyss.

The maid servant made it, coming out of the water feeling renewed, refreshed, and hungry. Burning before her was a fire. Its warmth comforted her. Near the flames were two small fish and some bread ready to eat. Without question, she knew who prepared it. She sat, ate, and had her fill.

After her meal, she noticed just off to the side and sitting under a tree, was battle armor complete with sword and shield. She was not skilled in weaponry or combat, but she was determined to get in the fight.

She camped for the night. In the morning, she would venture into the forest, fully prepared, in search of Princess Elise.

# Chapter 15

### The Husband/The King

Eli arrived just outside the castle. It was heavily guarded. He had no weapons, no plan. He circled the castle looking to find a way in without alarming all of the king's soldiers. If he wanted to save his wife, he needed to be smart about it.

He found a place to hide in a horse stable until night fall. From his position, he could examine the movements of the guards at a side entrance. This entrance was the least guarded with only two armed soldiers.

The opportunity to act had come. He fastened a saddle to a horse. Attached to the saddle was a rope twenty feet long. At the end of the rope was a small makeshift wagon he put together, small enough for a child to sit on. He then filled it with hay and smashed a burning lantern on it.

The horse was quickly startled by the fire and it raced passed the two guards at the side entrance. This caused a disturbance among those in the area, leading the guards to follow and get distracted long enough for Eli to sneak in.

The castle was large and he had no way of knowing how to find his wife, let alone navigate passed the many guards walking about. Anytime a guard approached he would blend in to his surroundings for cover.

Eventually, he found his way to an area designated for the servants. This was his chance to blend in. None of them were alarmed because they were too preoccupied with their duties. He found a place he could pretend to work. There, along the spot he chose, was a little girl. He made conversation with her and asked where he could find the king. She told him.

Eli made his way to the king's private quarters. The entrance to the room was guarded by two soldiers. There was no going back for him. No more sneaking around.

Eli charged them. Both soldiers were caught by surprise. He jumped in the air and struck the closest guard, knocking him down. The other pulled out his sword, swung it in haste, and wildly missed. Eli then punched the soldier several times before taking the sword from him. Turning the sword on the guard, he took one swipe and managed to cut off his right ear. Trembling, the other ran away calling for reinforcements. This left the king's door unmanned. Eli quickly entered.

The room was large with a stairway leading to a balcony. The king was at the top of the stairs holding a knife to Sarai's throat.

"Sarai!" Eli shouted to her. She was visibly frightened, crying.

"Ah! The husband," the king yelled. "I've heard much about you. Thank you for taking care of my livestock. Unfortunately, my soldiers realized later they forgot one. They were merely bringing back that which is mine. To your right, you will find a nice gold chalice. I'm sure that will cover the cost of your cow."

"You are sadly mistaken," Eli replied, "I am here for my wife, nothing more. Rest assured, I will not leave here without her and if you value your life you will release her to me."

"I've never had this much trouble with cattle before. This is so much fun!"

Immediately, the door burst open with the king's men, armed and ready to strike Eli down. He was surrounded.

"I didn't realize how valuable she was," the king continued, "it is usually my custom to give it three days before I get to personally break in my wild animals. Three days with the horses just outside. Well…with all of this excitement, why wait? I think I'll make an exception for this one. Make it quick," he ordered his guards, "I wish to enjoy my new servant."

The soldiers obeyed their king and started their attack. First, with two at a time, they intended each strike to be a deathblow. Without having any training with a sword, Eli was surprised with how calm he was. He felt confident, strong…eager to fight.

He easily out maneuvered the first two soldiers. Taking only two swings, he maimed them both. He then picked up another sword and fought off up to four soldiers at a time. To slow them down he didn't work hard for the kill as they did; instead, he targeted their arms, hands, and legs. The soldiers made it easy for him because they were too wild in the fight. They left themselves overly exposed for his attacks and on more than one occasion they managed to strike each other.

Finally, there was only one soldier standing opposite Eli. It was the same one charged with collecting Eli's cattle, the same one who notice Sarai's beauty, and the same one to convince the king to take her. He was the one holding Sarai as her parents were murdered. Eli recognized his face and dropped his swords.

"Perhaps it is appropriate for you to bring an end to this?" Eli asked him.

"I saw you ride in on your horse, so *I* alerted the king. Though, I don't remember seeing one on your land when I came to visit. When I am through with you, I'll go back to your home and destroy what is left of it."

The soldier charged Eli with all his might. He took a big swing, but Eli dodged it. He was spun around by the miss, tripped over another guard on the ground, and landed on his own sword. Eli stood over him as he lay dying.

"There is no place in my Kingdom for cowards like you," he told him just before he died.

"Your Kingdom?" the king shouted out while laughing, "You may have bested twenty of my men, but more will come. I doubt you can stop a whole army."

"And where is this army of yours? Perhaps they secretly anticipate the death of their ruthless king? I do not see an army here."

Eli started up the steps.

"Again, I say to you, if you value your life you will release her. If you do so, I will allow you to live."

More guards entered the room. They looked at the carnage before them, stunned, and saw Eli as he slowly ascended toward the king. They didn't take action. They watched.

"What are you doing? Kill this man!" the king commanded them.

Still, they did not move. More gathered in the room to witness the fall of the tyrant.

"Your time is up," Eli said, "*I* am your King now."

The king knew he was defeated. He lowered the knife to his side and said calmly, "I will not die by the hand of some peasant boy, nor will I die as anything but king."

Suddenly, he stabbed Sarai in the stomach with his dagger. He took three steps back, unsheathed his sword, and fell on it, killing himself.

"No!" Eli shouted.

He ran to his wife before she collapsed and held her in his arms. He rested on the floor with her, crying, suddenly hopeless and in complete despair.

"I cannot lose you too," he told her.

"The baby," she whispered, "our baby."

Eli looked at her wound and suddenly realized he was about to lose his family.

"If only there was a way, anything," he thought, when immediately he remembered the fig.

He pulled out the once bitten fruit.

"My love, take this. It may sooth your pain."

He put it to her mouth and she was able to take a small bite. With the little strength she had, she smiled and whispered, just before falling asleep, "I feel better already."

Soldiers approached them carefully.

"My King," one of them said, "it would be wise to let someone tend to her wounds."

"Very well," Eli responded.

The soldiers carefully took her. Physicians and servants were called to attend to her night and day until she was restored to better health.

### Promises

It took a couple of months before Sarai could walk again. During this time, Eli and Sarai were announced as the new King and Queen.

Eli was eager to reassure his Kingdom he would not be like his predecessor. He would be a fair King, only looking to bring peace to all the lands. Although he was their King, he reminded them he would be just. For he knew the hardships and struggles they faced because he too faced them before.

One night, the new King and Queen sat arm in arm overlooking their Kingdom.

"We will try again," she said. "We will have a princess...Princess Elise."

"*If* we have a princess, that will be her name, and what a beautiful name that is. But what about having a mighty prince?" he said jokingly.

"We can have both...and more like we've always planned," she said with excitement.

"I promise."

On the same night, while the Queen slept, the King stared out at everything before him. It was then he noticed the forest seemed much closer than before. It was odd but not enough to deter his sense of fulfillment.

"It has all come as I said, did it not?" an old familiar voice said.

"Ah, it is you," the King responded, "I've been waiting, at least wondering how I might find you to repay what you did for my wife and me."

"Yes, there is payment to be made, as I said before, there is."

"Name your price. I am willing to give you half of my Kingdom if you ask."

"Please, no need, none for me. I have my own. It must do for now."

"You have your own kingdom? Where is it so I know my ally?"

"It is in the forest not far from here, behind the trees. We will be linked."

"What kind of kingdom do you speak of?"

"Some might consider it a prison, but every now and then even prisoners find a way to escape."

The King did not know what to make of what she was saying so he moved on from the conversation.

"So, what is it you seek?"

"Your firstborn child," she said without hesitation. The King was beside himself.

"How can you ask for such a price as this?"

"Now, now, my King. You and your wife said you will have many. Who knows? Perhaps you need my assistance to have them as well, me alone. Besides, it is done. I do not need your permission to take the child, none at all. The child is mine and I will be back after it is born."

The King fell to his knees. Realizing the consequence of the decision he made in haste and knowing the witch's power to be great, he was seized with remorse.

"What have I done?"

"Do not fret; you will be a powerful King. By name alone you will rule this Kingdom, alone. Should you choose to make attempts to go back on our arrangement, I will take it all; you will have nothing once more, nothing."

"Then take it back now! Please! I've betrayed my wife!"

"And what is that to me?" she said coldly, "A life of wealth and no worries, you already decided. It is done. Your responsibility is to me now."

Before the King could get out his next words, the witch gave a laugh similar to a shriek and vanished into the night.

The King was so distraught he questioned his sanity. He knew he could not let her take his child. He could not destroy his family, the one he and his Queen desperately desired. The life they envisioned was gone.

He could not live with himself betraying his wife and their child. He felt hopeless, defeated.

He did not think she would ever forgive him if she were to find out, so he hid the truth. To do so, he kept himself busy. Always planning, going to war, and overseeing monuments erected in his honor. Although she would go along with him in his travels, he constantly avoided contact with her.

In these travels, he came across a man with poisons to suppress women from bearing children. The poisons would have a lasting effect and could result in women becoming completely barren. He purchased them in secret, thinking he would never be desperate enough to deceive his wife a second time.

Still, he could not stand the heartbreak in the face of his Queen when he thought of the day the witch would take their child. The face of horror in her eyes as she looked into his; the betrayal, the guilt. It was too much for him to consider. It didn't end there. He could not stomach thinking of what the witch might possibly do to his child. He would be powerless, so he turned to using the poisons.

Slowly, as the years passed, the King grew cold toward his wife. It started with hating himself, but he turned his bitterness against her. Not long after, the bitterness turned into resentment. He pushed her love away for so long he forgot why he did it in the first place. He was a new man, no longer the one she married.

Still, she always believed he would return to her. She fought off ill thoughts such as she would have been better off dying when she was stabbed. She knew he resented her. She blamed it on her inability to carry a child.

To keep herself busy, the Queen did all she could to think about others and use her position to help those in need. She could not allow herself to think it had all been for nothing and concluded there was something more for her to do. Still, she longed for bringing a child into the world with the man she loved her whole life.

# Chapter 16

**Strong and Courageous**

On the night of their first meeting, the sparrow educated Elise concerning her parents, Hope, and love. She had many questions and the sparrow gave her many answers. It was difficult at first, but the burning feeling inside of Elise helped her to believe and renewed her mind.

The following morning, the witch stormed the room.

"Wake up, orphan, time to wake up. No food for you, not now," she said before removing the stitches. The witch took Elise outside and had her lie down on one of the large stones sitting around a small fire.

Roots and vines grew out from the ground, pinning Elise to the stone. Her whole body, head to toe, was tied down. The witch said nothing to her. Instead, she focused her attention on the small fire. She stood close to it, raised her arms, and chanted in words unfamiliar to Elise.

The color of the fire slowly changed as the heat intensified. The smoke grew denser, black, slowly turning into a rising whirlwind.

Elise was amazed at what she saw, but she was also scared. The whirlwind shot into the morning sky, quickly overcoming and darkening it. The hotness started to burn the Princess so she cried out in agony. The louder she screamed, the more frightening the whirlwind grew. Suddenly, flashes of lightening danced within the black flurry.

One bolt jumped out to strike Elise. Her screams were deafening. However, just as quickly as it started, it was over. The smoke descended, allowing the light to show itself once more. The vines and roots holding the

Princess down also retreated back into the earth. They were no longer required as Elise passed out, exhausted.

In the late hours of the night, after having slept the day away, the Princess opened her eyes towards the high window. There sat the sparrow, crying.

"Why do you cry?" asked Elise in her thoughts, her mouth now sewn shut.

"No child should suffer as you do now."

"Do not worry sparrow, Hope will make it better."

"Yes child, it is as you say."

"Will you please tell me more stories about my parents?"

The sparrow told her stories, always reassuring her of the day they would all be together again. This was Hope's promise to her. Though, for now, she must endure suffering for a little while.

All of these events took place for six nights in a row. The seventh, according to the witch, would be the last.

"Tomorrow is my final day, friend," Elise told the sparrow, "I do wish I had enough strength to stand and see the moon one last time. Even if Hope does not help tomorrow, he will help me in death."

"My dear child, your time has not yet come. Tomorrow you will witness the power of Hope. He cannot fail. The cost is too great. Should the witch succeed, the sky will remain black, children in all the lands will perish, and Hope will be lost until the next childbirth. This is her purpose and she will make sure a child is never born again. There will be much pain and suffering until the world is completely desolate, all lost. The moon is in fact beautiful, but it is dark and unseen without the light of the sun. There must be light in these lands and you will be that light. But there cannot be salvation without forgiveness."

Princess Elise did not understand the full meaning of what she was told, but she cherished it in her heart and it gave her much needed comfort.

"I must leave now my Princess and join the ranks with your father, for tomorrow will be a great battle. Be strong and courageous. Hope will not disappoint you."

# Chapter 17

**Light vs. Dark**

The rabbit led the King down another path where he found his armor, ready for war.

"You will need this," the rabbit told him, "it has been over eight years now, lying here, waiting for you to become the man fit to wear it."

"Why did it take me so long?" the King asked.

"There is no shame over how long it has taken you. What matters is you are here now."

The King examined the armor before putting it on. It was light, like nothing he had worn before. He could feel every muscle in his body strengthen. After picking up his sword and shield he eagerly asked, "How much longer must I wait?"

"Not long. In fact, the witch's army is making their way to you now."

"An army!"

"Yes, but fear not…"

Suddenly, out of the dark corners of the forest stepped forward different creatures. There were rabbits, sparrows, wild dogs, mice, and brown bears; all on the side of Hope.

"…you are not alone. As I said before," the rabbit continued, "Hope is with you. As long as you have Hope, you can fight."

"And will Hope be here as well?"

"Look around you. You are surrounded by His presence. Perhaps one day you will meet face to face, but not today. You do not need to see his face to know he exists, remain faithful."

Upon saying this, a crow loudly made its presence felt as it flew dangerously close by. It rested on the ground not far from where the King stood.

"Caw, CAW!!!"

Immediately, the sounds of many crows flying through the trees were heard. They sat high in them, so numerous, they blocked out much of the light shining through. Then the others showed up: snakes, wolves, and black bears. The witch's legion quickly multiplied, eventually outnumbering their counterpart. Like two great walls, the armies stood opposite one another.

"Hope is little, not much with so little," the old familiar voice said.

The witch stepped out of the dark, amongst her villains.

"Perhaps it is time for you to die, your time. I have had my fun for so long, such fun, I forgot you were here," she told the King.

"Five hundred to one, our odds are still better with Hope," said the rabbit.

"All of this will be pointless come tomorrow, all. I will accomplish what I need to destroy Hope. You of course will be dead, of course, as will your precious daughter, dead. She has served me well, so strong," she teased with a wicked smile.

The King, like a madman, gave out a loud battle cry and charged the witch. If he could strike her down, it would all be over, but she vanished just before he could reach her, leaving him staring face to face with a roaring black bear. This was the beginning of the battle.

All of the creatures charged toward the opposing side, both eager to advance their kingdoms. The King carried his shield faithfully, blocking the strikes from the black bear, but before he knew it, he was pinned down, cornered between two trees. Everything was moving very quickly. The dark beast went for the kill, but a brown bear intervened and removed the menace with all of its might.

Now free and in the middle of the fray, the King looked around to see the creatures fight fiercely to the death. A crow flew within inches of his face. The surprise turned him around to see several more flying fast towards him. He got down on one knee and shielded himself.

The crows, in their berserker state, penetrated his shield with their beaks. One even managed to scrape the King's arm. Not a bad cut, but enough to let him know he needed to take the offensive.

With one swipe of his sword, he removed the stuck crows. He jumped back into the battle and, blow by blow, he struck down his enemies.

### Fair Warning

Although most of the creatures of Hope were not known to be as fierce as those of the witch, they found success by working together as a team.

The sparrows were particularly clever in their tactics as they flew in large circles, outside the hostilities, in order to attack unsuspecting crows from behind by lodging their beaks into the backs of their heads.

Many of the smaller animals could not be overlooked by their enemies. The mice climbed up the trees and jumped onto different foes all at once. They attacked in multitudes and their many bites to the neck would either kill their target or distract them long enough for their larger allies to come in for the finish.

Hope's army had the upper hand until the arrival of Abaddon. It flew in and there was an immediate turning point for the dark creatures. It was not to be outmatched. It was fast and brutally strong. Two brown bears approached it on both sides. They charged, but it didn't move. It waited. The moment they touched Abaddon, the beast extended its arms, punching through their chests, killing them instantly.

The King, in all of his fearlessness, charged Abaddon, but was struck by its wing, sending him thirty feet away.

"I could have killed you King, just now," Abaddon said to him, "I will still, it is my nature, by order of the witch."

"And yet, you stand there to simply gloat?" the King responded, hurting as he stood back up.

"I've been in this prison long enough, too long. While I cannot keep myself from killing, I've learned to delay it, if only for a little while."

"Why do you choose to delay it with me?"

"It is important to understand how I learned to delay my appetite, and that is, I accepted my fate. I've hated the witch for a long time and solely blamed her, but it was I alone, my arrogance, my decisions led me to become this…monster. *I* killed my family."

"You were a man once?"

"Yes. Just like you, I was a husband and father. I do not wish to see you fall into the same fate as...argh...as... I."

"How do you know of such things?"

"I am blind, but I see fine. I have knowledge of the forest, of the witch, and your daughter."

"Then, please, help me save her!"

"I...grrr...will. And so, you must know, this fight will be to the death. My ...aannnimal instinctssss... are taking over and I ...wwill lose control. I cannot hear what ...doesssn't ...mooove. You must trick my ...ssense of ...ssmmmell."

"I do not understand."

"You ...mmusssst ...kkillll, ...AARGh... me if youuu wish to ...ssee yyour girlll ...agggainnn ...GRRRR!"

222

Abaddon lost total control. He gave a loud roar and charged forward in the direction he knew the King to be.

The brute lunged fast, wings spread to their fullest, claws ready to tear apart the man. The King managed to dodge the first attempt on his life. He threw himself to his right, rolling into a standing position. He saw Abaddon destroy the base of a tree with the strike intended for him. The King quickly turned to run.

A wolf, hidden in the chaos, leaped out hoping to attack the King, but a rabbit countered with a mighty leap of its own, striking the wolf underneath the jaw and knocking it out of the fight.

"If we want to win," the rabbit shouted to the King, "you must defeat the monster. It will pursue you, and never give up its purpose in destroying you."

The King looked back toward Abaddon. He saw it surveying the battle with its senses, hoping to track the

King. With a giant leap, it flew up into the trees and was out of sight.

"You mustn't give up on Hope," the rabbit continued, "we are all here fighting the same fight. Now go! You must set a trap. We will keep the fight here."

The rabbit jumped back into battle and so the King continued to run, stopping only to fend off attacks, until he was finally alone.

## To the Death

The King stopped in a clearing encircled by trees when he heard a crackling of broken twigs. He drew his sword, but it was not Abaddon stepping towards him, it was the maid servant.

"My King!" she shouted out as she removed her helmet.

"It is you," he responded surprisingly, "I know you. You were a servant in my castle; one of the Queen's favorites."

"Yes, your majesty. It is as you say."

"But…what brings you here, and in full battle armor, none the less?"

"I am here to fight with you, to save the Princess, your daughter."

"How is it you know of her?"

"I was there when she was born. I was there when your wife gave her own life for this child, Princess Elise."

King Eli, having heard his daughter's name for the first time, grew weak in his knees. She was the promise he tried to withhold from his wife.

"She should have been conceived out of love, not bitterness and strife," he confessed with a heavy heart.

"And yet, she is still your daughter and she is waiting for you. I am here to keep my promise to the Queen, a promise I will give my life to fulfill."

Suddenly, there was a roar in the distance. The King could sense it getting closer. He started to think quickly and examined the trees encircling them.

"Trick my sense of smell," the King said recalling what Abaddon told him earlier.
The King cut his hand and placed the blood on all of the surrounding trees.

"What is it you are doing?" the maid servant asked confusingly.

"We must trick the creature's sense of smell."

"What is it you are trying to trick? What creature?" she asked with alarm.

"It is a blind creature that talks as if there is a man trapped within it."

"Abaddon! It is real? I thought it was just an old story," she said surprised and frightened.

"We do not have time to compare stories. It will find us soon. Now, quickly do as I do."
The maid servant did. All of the trees surrounding them were then marked with their blood.

"When it arrives, you must hold still and breathe as little as possible. Any movements will direct its attention at you."

"King!!!" Abaddon shouted abruptly just before landing in the middle of the clearing. It inhaled strongly, searching for the King's scent.

"I can smell your blood around me. I will taste it and then eat your..." it stopped short of his words and breathed in deeply once more. "There is another here with you. This will simply not do King. This was a valiant effort, but I ...knnnow the ...diffferrrence. Urgh. Your ...bblood flows and ...youuu have a stronger scent ...wwith an open ...wwound ...sssuch as the one you ...hhave. GRRr. My body ...wwill decide which ...tto ...kkilll ...ffirrr ...GGRRR ...ssstt. RROOARRRRR!"

Abaddon went after the one closest to it, the maid servant. She was smart to have kept a tree between her and Abaddon. It struck the tree and knocked it over; now it rested on another ready to fall completely on any moment's notice.

The King positioned himself behind a tree, as well, and gave a loud shout to get its attention. Abaddon flew towards him and once again, damaged the tree instead.

The maid servant, seeing the opportunity to strike, but with no knowledge of how fierce Abaddon was in a fight, charged. However, before she could stab it from behind, the creature slapped her whole body with its wing, knocking her far back, half conscious, and incapable of defending herself.

"Do not cry out in pain," Abaddon told her, "for I can hear you. It is easier for me to kill you if I hear you. Smelling …bblood around …sstill throws off my sense of …ssmell, even if for a …moment."

Abaddon tried to contain itself. The Butcher, still inside, fought as best he could to hold back. This caused the monster to convulse. Its roar cracked as if it were in pain and crying out.

The King seized the moment. He ran towards the leaning tree as it was aligned with where Abaddon stood. He gave it the push needed to send it crashing over for good. The tree smashed onto the shoulders of Abaddon, pinning it down to the ground.

The maid servant managed to sit up as best she could while the King approached Abaddon carefully. The creature snarled quietly in pain. It could no longer move; its back was shattered by the impact. Slowly, the growls died off and the man's voice returned.

"Thank you," he said, "I have carried this burden long enough. Perhaps there is Hope for me yet."

"There is," the King reassured.

"Then, please…free me once and for all."

The King took his sword with both hands and thrust it through Abaddon's heart. Immediately, a mist, consumed the body of the creature. So much so, the King and maid servant could no longer see it.

As quickly as it appeared, it faded away and there stood the Butcher, back to his human form, water dripping all over.

"Thank you, friend," he told the King.

Out of the woods, two young children ran towards the Butcher; the same young children the King saw when he sat tied to a tree.

"Papa! Papa!" they shouted with joy.
The children embraced their father.

"I wish I could join your fight," the Butcher lamented.

"No," the King responded quickly, "it is long overdue for you to be with your family. May you go in peace."

"And may you one day reunite with yours as I."

The Butcher turned around, carrying both of his children towards his wife, waiting to greet him. Slowly, they walked off together vanishing into the forest.

The rabbit, familiar to the King, hobbled toward him injured.

"The battle is won for now," he said.

The King was still staring in the direction of where the Butcher and his family walked off to.

"The forest is ours," said the King, "now…let's go rescue my daughter."

The King, instinctively, ran up to a tree and started to climb. He made his way to the very top. From there, he could see the vast forest, but more importantly, he could see the smoke rising from the home of the witch. It was a long walk ahead, but he did not plan on walking.

# Love

# Chapter 18

### **Killing Fields**

Back when King Greedy first took control of the Kingdom, he employed the servants necessary to keep his castle intact. It was important for him to maintain his personal livestock as well as the gardens, especially the vineyards, to feed his appetite of constant consumption. He relished every bite, every sip, celebrating his reign with indulgence.

There was a family charged with maintaining the livestock and overseeing the hundreds working the land. Within this family was a young boy named Joshua.

Since they were already employed there before King Greedy took over, they were kept on. He had them, as with all of his servants, swear their allegiance. They did so out of fear for they quickly knew he was not a man of mercy.

During the first two years under King Greedy's reign, this family was protected. The new king did not want anyone else in charge. Their work had to be perfect and anyone else trying to do their job would not be good enough. Unfortunately for the family, this would change. King Greedy began to lose interest in the day to day activities within his castle walls and around the Kingdom. As long as his cravings were gratified, it didn't matter how. He no longer desired perfection and valued quantity over quality. This was the beginning of instability and danger for those working for him.

Soon enough, the family in charge of the livestock would see first-hand the desperation within the Kingdom. In the beginning stages, the mere threat of the king's name would chase away the bandits. It was enough to scare those trying to go unseen. Eventually, the bandits didn't care; they and their families were as good as dead anyway.

Their outcry to the king about the bandits fell on deaf ears. The only response from him regarding the livestock was to maintain their quota. It was up to them to defend themselves, their positions, and their livelihood; anyone working for the king received lodging and daily meals for themselves and their immediate family members. Their jobs were coveted by those on the outside looking in, and soon bandits were not just interested in stealing food, but they wanted the jobs of those in the fields. And it was much easier to take someone's place outside the castle than inside; one could not simply walk in or they *would* be killed.

For this to be accomplished, it was as straightforward as a bandit sneaking onto the fields, killing a worker, and taking over their duties. They would just as easily take their lodging as well. If they didn't kill the immediate family members too, they would run them off and replace them with their own. King Greedy didn't care, he just wanted his quota.

## **Shepherd**

Joshua's father put him in charge of overseeing the sheep and the other sheep herders. Even at his young age he was very skilled as a shepherd. The sheep knew his voice well and trusted him as he had to protect them from the occasional wild animal. Still, it wasn't the wild animals he needed to be afraid of. His youth made him vulnerable to attacks. It didn't take a man of great intellect to understand this.

In their best efforts to protect themselves, his family stayed in close proximity with each other, at least within eye sight. It was a necessary precaution, but having to make these adjustments slowed their work days as well as the efficiency of their duties, all the while, still needing to meet their quota.

Five years past and the family had defended themselves from multiple attacks. Unfortunately, one of these encounters resulted in the mother's death. After the bandit killed her, the family buried her in the late evening. Joshua's older brother wanted to kill the man out of revenge, but his father convinced him not to. The man had taken over the duties of their mother and they needed the extra hand if they wanted to meet the demands of the king. This was the new way of trying to survive and without the help of the unwanted stranger, they all faced death. It was a cruel conundrum, a necessary evil, and so the rage of Joshua's brother boiled.

The days turned to weeks having to work alongside a man they hated. One evening, Joshua's brother snuck out of their lodging and stabbed the man to death while he slept. He stayed up all night burying the body to hide what he did. The next morning, they were shorthanded and ordered by the king to surrender many of the best livestock for a large feast he wanted to have. To make matters worse, he only gave them the afternoon to have all of the preparations ready. Without the extra help, they fell short of the order and the king was outraged. He didn't care for excuses. At first, he wanted to kill them, but instead, he banished Joshua's father and brother. He reasoned it would be fitting to bring them misery before their eventual deaths outside the castle walls. He kept Joshua on as an added insult to separate the family. Furthermore, this isolated Joshua, leaving him susceptible to an attack on any given day.

"You will leave here knowing this boy will die in due time and there is nothing you can do about it," King Greedy told them.

So, his family was gone, exiled. Any attempt to rescue the boy would bring certain death to all of them.

Joshua was alone and suspicious of the people brought in to manage the livestock for they were part of a bigger family. The only problem they had, he thought, was after they killed him, which of their family members would take his place. He had some time on his side though because they needed him to show them how things were done. They were nice and treated him kindly until they started gaining confidence in themselves and their productivity. As their self-reliance became more common, their aggression toward Joshua grew.

His usefulness to them was almost over, and to prevent his impending death, Joshua made a deal. They only needed his spot and didn't need to kill him for it. He volunteered to give this up and they welcomed the idea. However, they didn't simply let him leave. They decided he needed to stay on, without lodging and without his standard share of the food. Joshua was forced to work and only given bread and water sparingly. So, he did what he was told, slept chained under a tree alongside his sheep, and kept to himself.

He often fell asleep thinking of his family. He missed them and wondered what became of his father and brother. He wanted to leave and find them, but he wasn't ready to go out on his own. So, for the next year, Joshua built himself up; labored harder than any two men combined and was determined to win over everyone working alongside him.

Not long after, the same family eager to push Joshua out, changed their minds and went out of their way to make space for him. They no longer treated him as an outsider. Instead, they highly regarded him and even sacrificed their own meals, if need be, so he could have his fill. Some even had a rotation to skip meals so he could have their portion. He was becoming a man, a leader.

### Through the Fog Together

King Eli charged through the forest riding atop a brown bear. He was determined to find the witch and save the Princess. They were ahead of all the others. Not too much longer did his nostrils begin to sting as the smell of burning sulfur made its way in. Black ash floated across the path before him so he knew he was close and could expect to run into the witch at any moment.

However, a fog started slowly before him and soon took the appearance of a solid wall. It was so dense he could not see his hand passed it. King Eli dismounted the bear and considered his options.

"Take heed, King," the bear cautioned, "perhaps, it is best to not go it alone?"

"Every second guess I waste brings my daughter closer to death. I shouldn't care about what happens to me. I should jump in right now!"

"You are no longer a coward, King, so now isn't the time to be foolish. Do not be too hasty just to prove yourself brave. Do not let yourself be controlled by your anger; anger labels you a fool. This is a moment to exercise wisdom."

The King thought about the advice and decided the bear was right.

"It is as you say. We should wait for the others to catch up so we can all go together. We will be stronger for it."

"Sorry, my King, but that is not how it works. We cannot join you against the witch."

"Then why should I wait if I am alone in this fight?"

"You are not alone. Your maid servant is making her way here and will arrive shortly. Pity the man that falls and has no one to pick him up. You will need each other to get through the fog, for you, it is the only way." Finally, the others arrived.

"Is there a problem?" the maid servant asked as she dismounted from the bear she was riding.

"They cannot go in with us. They cannot fight the witch."

"Well, I am here," she replied without hesitation, "we can do it together."
Her confidence became his.

They armed themselves with sword and shield before approaching the fog.

"This will not be a simple walk through," the rabbit said, "you are stepping into dark magic, her magic. The witch will expose your fears and use them against you. It will not be enough for only one of you to overcome them. You must both do it, only then will you break her spell and make it out of the fog."

King Eli and the maid servant looked at each other, took a deep breath and stepped into the abyss.

## One Last Time

Princess Elise lay in her bed with little strength, exhausted from the previous six days. As tired as she was, she was unable to sleep though she was desperate to dream again of the woman smiling. The Princess longed to see her, to be at peace. With this in mind she thought, "Perhaps I could fall asleep one last time, never to wake up again, and be with her?"

As each of the previous days ended, the witch seemed more and more excited, almost like a child. A contributing factor to Elise's insomnia was the witch's constant laughing; echoing throughout the walls, her voice was piercing. When she wasn't laughing, the Princess could hear the witch speaking by herself and maybe even to herself.

"Will you be there?" Elise thought, as if asking the woman. "When I die, I want you to be there."

The door suddenly burst open. The witch had her crooked smile, still laughing.

"Yes, my pet, there you are, such misery, there. All I need, I can feel it all. No time to waste, up, get up. One more time, all will end for you, what you want. Oh, how I've waited, patiently waited."

The witch needed to hurry for she was fully aware of King Eli's victory and his approach through the fog. Using her magic, she gave life to the bed Elise was on and it carried her outside. The bed took her and placed her on the cold stone one last time.

# Chapter 19

### **Together**

King Eli and the maid servant walked cautiously in the fog, anticipating the witch's magic. Without knowing it, they were separated. Now alone trekking through the heavy, seemingly endless, fog, the trial of the witch began:

Their thoughts were hazy, as if suddenly awakened after a long slumber. Hallucinations accompanied their sins laid before them; guilt, betrayal, selfishness, cowardice…all played a role to get them here. Their insecurities and fears were on full display.

The whispers started:

"There is no Hope…"

"Your Queen is dead…"

"Blood on your hands…"

"You have already failed…"

"Hope has failed you…"

"You will die here, alone…"

Soon, they were overwhelmed by the sounds of crows attacking and snakes hissing at their feet. They were taunted with laughter, shouts of pain, and accusation:

"You lied to me!!"

"AARGGHHH!!"

"You abandoned your family!"

"You did this!"

"You killed me!"

In desperation, they did the best they could to drown out the noise.

The witch did not stop there. She forced them to see their biggest regrets and the shameful moments in their past projected within the fog all around. They saw the worst of themselves and the hurt they caused others.

Suddenly, their hands were engulfed in flames, both now screaming in agony. They fell to their knees trying to put out the fires, slamming their hands on the ground.

"It is no use…"

"Only death awaits you…"

"Hope does not exist here…"

"You cannot overcome with Hope…"

They were defeated. The witch's magic was too powerful. Still, something about what they heard, one of the whispers, stayed with them, "You cannot overcome with Hope…"

It was as if a needle was piercing their hearts, these words repeating over and over. Although separated, they frantically tried to understand why these words were drawing them in.

Suddenly, they both said, "You're right!"

They were not there with Hope; Hope only brought them together.

They stood up at the same time, hands still on fire, and in their own way overpowered their fear. Each defiantly spoke out against the witch and made sure she understood she was wrong. It was not Hope giving them strength, nor was it Hope driving them to fight through their darkest moments, their deepest regrets. It was because of love they were there, for they knew nothing was more powerful. Only because of love were they willing to risk their lives. Hope may have helped them get there, but it would be love getting them through.

As they were talking, their voices began to slowly cut through the fog and soon, they were able to hear each other. The flames died down, the fog dissipated, and the pain subsided. There they stood, side by side, and they embraced in relief.

"Ah, the King and his servant here to die, here," the old familiar voice said as the rest of the fog cleared to reveal their arrival.

## A Mother's Love

There she was. The witch was levitating behind a small fire as a whirlwind rose from the flames. The Princess lay motionless, tied on top of a stone. She was half conscious, not knowing if she was awake or still dreaming.

"Release her!" the King demanded.

"Now why would I do that, why?" the witch replied. "You may have found a way out of my fog, but your love has no effect on me."

"My sword will have its effect on you!"

The King and maid servant charged forward, but they were no match for the witch's power. Out of the whirlwind, lightning shot out all around the two. They defended as best they could with their shields.

Blasts of power eventually knocked them to the ground where they were quickly wrapped up in vines and roots. The witch laughed, and there was nothing else they could do.

Suddenly, one of the large stones nearby shook violently, cracking down on all sides, splitting into limbs, a torso, a head; becoming a rock monster designed for death.

Elise, still in her daze, was unaware of what was happening. Her head was resting, turned to her right. Through tired eyes, she could see the blurred silhouette of a woman standing nearby. Time seemed to stand still for her, for this moment. Everything else came to a halt. Elise questioned whether she finally died and the woman was there to welcome her.

Eventually, her sight was restored and she could see the woman clearly. She was beautiful. The woman approached Elise and held her hand. Feeling her touch, Elise knew immediately who she was. Her mother, the same woman from her dreams, was there. Their connection gave her peace and the same fleeting sensation she only felt by their yearly communion.

Queen Sarai looked into her daughter's eyes, both now in tears, and with such kindness said, "*This* is love, and you are loved."

"I've dreamt about you," Elise said.

"And I, you. You are more beautiful now than the first time I held you. And just like I knew then, you are strong, and so brave."

"Am I going to die? I want to be with you."

"Someday you will, but not today. There is darkness in the world and you must first be its light. But to do so, you must not hold on to the pain, the confusion. Any anger that lingers because of the life you have had to endure, you need to be willing to let it go."

"I am willing," the Princess replied.

Suddenly, the vines loosened and released their hold on Elise. The Princess had strength again and jumped off of the stone unbeknownst to the witch still fixated on the King and maid servant. Elise ignored the fight and made her way to the witch.

The witch, laughing as her rock creature was ready to kill the King, suddenly gasped in horror. She watched helplessly as her monster crumbled upon itself, the whirlwind in the fire dematerialized, and the King and maid servant were released from their entanglement, no longer in danger. The witch's power had been undone. She looked down to her left and saw Elise holding her cloak.

"Child, what have you done, what?" the witch cried out in terror.

"I forgive you."

The witch fell to the ground in agony knowing she lost.

Both the King and maid servant stood in awe. Elise saw them and slowly approached, stopping ten feet from the King. Their eyes met for the first time and the King dropped to his knees, speechless. After eight years of rehearsing what he would say to her, the moment he fought and nearly died for was finally here. Still, nothing could have prepared him for it.

"Are you my father?" she asked.

The King was choked up, tears rolling down his cheeks. He couldn't think of any words. All he could think of was how much she looked like her mother. It was a simple question requiring a simple answer. He nodded.

Elise, now crying too, was finally free. Eight years of torment, exhaustion, and sadness came out all at once and she ran to him for their first embrace.

"Oh, my sweet Elise," he finally said.

King Eli didn't need to understand what happened with the witch. He no longer needed the confrontation so he left her in her pitiful state. She was no longer a threat. They won. The maid servant stood by, giving them the moment eight years in the making; a family finally united.

# Chapter 20

### **Witness**

For his own entertainment, King Greedy would bring desperate men into a small arena he constructed on his fields. Once inside, these men were given a sword and shield. Sometimes, there would be as many as five at a time, armed and ready to fight. All they had to do was defend themselves long enough to survive the onslaught of one of King Greedy's dead soldiers. Should they survive the allotted time set by an hour glass, they could be rewarded with food and additional provisions to give to their families. Of the countless men who stumbled in, none ever came out alive. As they died, they were added to King Greedy's army.

A young man stepped forward, confidently. He understood the price, but his sister was starving, he had to try. With sword and shield in hand, the young man was ready and King Greedy turned the hour glass.

The young man's strategy was simple: avoid the advances of the dead soldier. He was quick and agile, doing somersaults to avoid the death strikes. To help him stall for time, he would target the legs of the dead soldier and even managed to cut one off. This slowed it down significantly, but it was still very dangerous.

After leaping away from another strike, the young man landed on his ankle awkwardly, twisting it. As he lay in pain, the dead soldier cornered him. The creature approached, hopping on one good leg, when the young man kicked it out from under, bringing living corpse down with a heavy thud. Instinctively, the young man stabbed the creature with his sword and scurried as fast as he could to get away before it got back up. King Greedy was amused by the turn of events until he realized something was wrong. His monster wasn't moving. For the first time in eight years, King Greedy was struck with fear. Even the young man was astonished. He looked to the hour glass as the last bit of sand dropped. The time was up. He survived.

As the young man celebrated, King Greedy rose from his seat and walked over to examine the body closely…no movement, no life. He stood back up and stared out into the forest. As much as he didn't want to, he needed to visit the witch.

"This is unbelievable!" the young man said to himself, loud enough for the king to hear.

"Yes, unbelievable!" King Greedy said annoyingly.

The king walked over to one of his guards and whispered into its ear. Immediately, another struck the young man down from behind. King Greedy stood over the boy, waiting for him to turn, to join the ranks of the Dead, but he never did. Regardless, the king could not have allowed the young man to live or he would risk word spreading throughout the lands about what happened: the soldiers were no longer immortal and the dead were not rising to serve him.

Near the arena was Joshua working with the animals, and he happened to hear the young man when he was celebrating. The commotion led Joshua to be a witness to the events. He knew it would not be long before King Greedy began to inquire of those working in the fields to see if anyone heard or saw anything in the arena that afternoon. It would be likely for others to point to Joshua as a possible witness since he was in the area tending to his flock as he did every day at that very hour. He had no choice but to flee immediately and avoid sharing the news with anyone in and around the castle.

The truth he obtained was much too delicate and dangerous. Like a priceless treasure he stumbled upon, he needed to protect it with his life.

Joshua set out on a journey to find others he could trust, others like him, ready to stand up to King Greedy and his dead army. Victory was possible, he just needed to show them.

## **Friend**

After defeating the witch, King Eli carried his daughter through the forest alongside the maid servant. He had so much adrenaline, he felt as though he could carry her forever. The Princess had her arms wrapped around him while she rested her head on his shoulder, asleep.

"Thank you," he said to the maid servant, "the Queen was very fond of you and your mother. I now know why."

"That is very kind of you my Lord…"

"No," he interrupted, "do not call me that. I will no longer look at you as a servant, but as a friend. So please, address me as such. Call me Eli."

"As you wish…Eli," she said awkwardly.

"And what should I call you? I'm sorry, I am embarrassed to say, I do not even know your name."

"It is Miriam."

"Very well…Miriam."

"I remember the first time I saw you," Miriam said. "I was a little girl then, but I remember. I was there when you snuck into the castle to save your wife. You asked me for directions."

"I…," he started as he recalled the memory of the past, "that…was you?"

"Yes," she said with a smile. "When it was first announced, you would be King, there was great excitement around the Kingdom. Knowing you were once a commoner like us. It gave us hope. You were a great King, and I know you will bring that same hope to all the lands again."

"And what of the Kingdom now? I know it was Greedy Fool that made a deal with the witch. I saw him standing, watching as his army tore through mine."

"The Kingdom is in ruins. The people are starving, desperate. King Greedy is ruthless and he enjoys watching everyone suffer while he, of course, has everything. Only those of us providing services to the king are well fed. Some think he needs servants to take care of him, but I think he keeps us around for the illusion of being a king."

"So, he has servants? Why hasn't anyone tried to poison him if they are giving him food to eat?"

"We are all afraid. He told us if he were to die at someone's hand, his dead army would kill everybody because they would be without a master to control them. They would just run wild. And when they kill, their victims are resurrected as immortal, soulless corpses moving about only to serve King Greedy. Should he die, the world would be full of the dead wandering aimlessly. All would be lost."

"There is always Hope," the Princess said silently as if she was talking in her sleep. "We will find a way."

As they approached the messengers of Hope waiting to greet them, the rabbit shouted out, "What a sight!"

"Thank you for your help," the King replied, "I wish desperately to turn around and live the rest of my days with my daughter hidden from the Kingdom, but there is still much to do. Much wrong that needs to be undone."

"Then let's get to it," the rabbit replied with confidence. "We know the witch's power has been removed. This means King Greedy's army is susceptible to being destroyed. We cannot just take him head on, not yet. We must build an army of our own and we must do it in secret, for his dead soldiers are scattered everywhere, always watching and reporting."

# Chapter 21

## **Always Greedy**

King Greedy ventured into the forest on a horse alone. He didn't worry about safe trails or having to face any dark creatures under the witch's spell. He wasn't harassed by any crows and there was no change in temperature; they had an agreement. Still, all was too calm. It was peaceful and it shouldn't have been.

The animals residing in the forest were not afraid. They gathered together in the open. A deer even walked in front of King Greedy without taking notice or showing alarm at his presence. He studied the forest: every movement, wind gust, and sound. His fear grew. If the witch's power had somehow been vanquished, his reign was in jeopardy. It would take an army just the right size to challenge him and he could lose everything. All it took was for someone to accidently kill a dead soldier. Word would then spread quickly and not long after, people would go for his head. He imagined being tortured; an opportunity for everyone to take a knife to him one at a time. He knew he deserved it.

King Greedy was holding on to his own kind of hope. Wanting a simple explanation from the witch, he rode his horse faster to get his answers more quickly.

After two and a half days, he arrived. Her home was quiet, surrounded by animals casually walking by, eating what they could find. The small fire was still going, but there was no black smoke and no sign of the witch. He did not call out. He only examined his surroundings before slowly entering her home. This was the first time anyone had done so willingly.

Her home was unimpressive. It contained six rooms, three on each side of one single hall. These rooms were small and bare, each simply containing a cot and window. In a couple of the rooms he saw what appeared to be etchings as well as other forms of markings scrawled on the walls. Some were to keep track of the days as they passed while others seemed like mental notes, names, and places someone didn't want to forget.

Finally, he made his way to the last room on the left. There she was, laying on the floor in a fetal position, looking as though someone kicked her in the stomach. She was moaning and writhing. For the first time, her veil was lifted and her whole face was exposed. Her eyes and forehead were grotesquely scarred.

"S…so close, mine, almost…no, she forgives, how? Close, so close," she whispered repeatedly to herself.

King Greedy watched her and, for once, was tempted to feel pity, but his anger consumed him.

"All that power," he said with such contempt, "and for what? Wasted on you! What is it you are whimpering on about?"

The witch, almost in hysterics, looking all over as if trying to fix her eyes on an object flying around, sat up and said, "The girl, she took it, gone. NOTHING MORE!"

"What girl?"

"The Princess…the Princess, little wretched child…so selfish!"

"How could you let a little girl defeat you? Is she powerful too? Does she have your magic?" he asked attempting to mask his fear of hearing the answer to his question.

"Must be powerful, her touch. Nothing like I felt before, nothing."

"And what of my army? Is this why they can be killed again?"

"Yes, killed once more, second death."

"Where is this Princess? If I kill her, will that change anything?"

"No, all is lost, gone…I do not know where…she took it!"

The witch was now sobbing and King Greedy was growing more impatient with her. His anger was setting in.

"Is there anything else?" he asked as he drew his sword slowly.

"Yes," she said, unaware of his intentions, "the King…he lives. He will come for you next, you like me…next."

King Greedy, now furious, impaled the witch with his sword.

"You are no longer of any use to me. You have broken our deal and the penalty is death."

The witch, now choking on her own blood was gasping for air, her eyes met King Greedy's as if she could see them.

"Don't look so surprised," he teased, "you should thank me. I'm putting you out of your misery as I would a sick dog."
He pulled his sword back and she fell over, eyes and mouth still wide, motionless.

King Greedy grabbed a lamp nearby and made his way outside toward the small fire. He examined the house for a loose piece of wood and broke it off. He poured the oil on from the lamp and set it ablaze. Then he proceeded with burning the house down. It caught quickly and was soon engulfed in flames with the witch still inside.

Finally, he kicked off a piece of burning wood, grabbing it from one end and casually walked to a nearby tree. He lit it on fire and continued to do so with every cedar surrounding the burning house.

He needed to find the King and Princess before they could challenge him. If they were hiding or still walking in the forest, a fire would force them out and perhaps one of his dead soldiers would spot them.

He was and had always been greedy and there was no cost too great to get what he wanted.

# Chapter 22

## **Call to Arms**

King Eli needed to build an army, but convincing people to fight could prove difficult. Having lived under King Greedy's rule, they were already subject to horrific circumstances. This changed them. They became desperate, paranoid, and there was a loss of empathy toward outsiders. Multitudes of people were too far gone from human decency, but King Eli knew they were still worth saving.

By defeating the witch, they did not allow darkness to overcome; light remained. There was still hope. Mere words would not be enough to completely convince the people to fight. King Eli anticipated this and knew he must show them.

Eli, Miriam, and Elise were accompanied by a group of Hope's creatures. Their plan was simple: remain hidden. As advised by the rabbit, they needed to stay within the edge of the forest line as they traveled to avoid the dead army picking up on the scent of a firstborn, the Princess. Keeping out of sight would allow them safe travel far away from the castle in search of a remote village guarded by only one dead soldier. King Eli would need to kill it in front of an audience to prove to the people it could be done. The killing needed to be swift and without detection to avoid the Dead communicating with each other about an uprising. This approach required a clever and careful plan.

After a four-day journey, they found a small village, but it was not the kind of place they anticipated it to be. It was located near the mouth of a river running far throughout all of the lands. Many skilled fishermen lived there and shared their daily catch with the community, and they were not lacking in food. The expression on the faces of the people did not reveal them to be downcast, but content. This place was almost a sanctuary, if not for the corpse walking and watching among them.

It was midday and everyone in the village kept busy outside with their chores. The dead soldier stood in the center of it all, ready to attack at a moment's notice; shield and sword firmly held. King Eli and his group scouted until Eli finally stepped out of the forest for the first time in eight years. The sun hit his face completely, blinding him for a moment, but it felt good. He took a little time to appreciate it before making his way to the dead soldier.

He almost went without being noticed by the villagers. Few caught a glimpse of the stranger and looked on as he picked up his pace, rapidly moving towards the guard whose back was turned. To their surprise, the man they watched drew his sword. One of the villagers understood what was about to happen.

"No!" the villager cried out.

His shout drew notice by some of the others still doing their chores, even the dead soldier, but before it could see what the commotion was King Eli pierced it through the back. The guard immediately collapsed by the blow, falling face down. The King stood over it, and cut off its head. He now had everyone's attention.

He could see the expressions on their faces. There was a mixture of confusion, amazement, and fear.

"Brothers and sisters," the King began as he stood over the corpse, "today is a new day. I have just proven to you we can now fight back. The magic in these lands have gone, you do not have to be afraid anymore."

A man stepped forward from the crowd, a blacksmith. His face was scarred and he wore a patch over his left eye.

"And how has this come to pass?" the blacksmith asked. "What do you know of such things? Who are you?"

"Before this madness plagued our lands, I was your King. I am King Eli, the Common." Immediately, murmurs began with some gasps of disbelief.

"Greedy Fool," the King started again, "made a deal with the witch of the forest. It was her magic that gave him his dead army. I stand here telling you it is over. I have faced the witch, and with the help of my family and Hope, she has been defeated."

The people remained stoic. Nobody was rejoicing as the King had anticipated. He was confused by the villager's apathy.

"Maybe you have," said the blacksmith, "but I've faced them myself. I barely survived; one of the one hundred spared to send a message to the rest of the Kingdom, to the world. I should have died amongst the thousands that fell at that Great War. Instead, I came here to help build what we now have. There are no firstborns among us, no fear of killing one of our own. We will live out our days as a community until we are no more. We have water, plenty of fish, and our land has improved tenfold for crop and farming. We've made a real life here under the circumstances. We should continue to lay low, keep to ourselves, and die in peace."

The people around him started shouting in agreement.

"But now you have brought trouble on us all!" the blacksmith shouted.

The crowd suddenly grew angry with the King. Some started calling out to have him tied up so they could hand him over to King Greedy, in hopes it might spare them his wrath.

Sensing the tension, Hope's creatures stepped out of the forest and made their way between the assemblage to stand by the King. All were now silent and many were amazed to see both a little girl and a woman riding on top of a brown bear. King Eli used this opportunity to speak.

"There is Hope yet," he said with a smile, "before you, is proof of this. You say you are at peace, yet, war is at hand. Do not shut your eyes and pretend it will go away. You have been living in fear, but you do not have to be afraid anymore. Brothers, you are not alone in this fight, *we* are not alone. Your swords will reveal the truth, just as mine has."

The King bent over to pick up the severed head, lifting it high for all to see, but there were no loud cheers, just silence. Some of the people had sad or horrific looks on their faces. Once again, the King was confused. Slowly, the crowd parted down the middle ending with an old man having fallen on his knees, hands covering his face, crying.

"It isn't as simple as you think," the blacksmith said somberly. "I do not know where you have been, but we do not see the dead as you do. You addressed us as brothers and sisters; *these* are our brothers and sisters, friends, neighbors, mothers and fathers. What you ask now is impossible. These aren't monsters to us, corpses with rotted flesh and bone like Greedy's first army. Those that have faced them, fallen in battle, have resurrected to serve King Greedy and he has them placed around their own communities for us to see, a reminder of what and who we've lost. Their appearance is like ours, save for their mortal scars and grey skin."

A few men approached King Eli slowly, one with a satchel, to retrieve the head. Two other men quietly carried the corpse away to be buried. Once again, the King lost his audience. The village was divided. Many wanted to fight, arguing they should honor their dead and release them from their dark forms. Some believed their dead relatives still felt pain and didn't want to harm them. Finally, others were afraid the souls of the Dead were trapped inside the corpses, having no control of their bodies. This meant they could see the horrors they inflicted on others; on those they loved and cared for.

During this debate, Elise slid off the bear and approached the old man on his knees, who was still mourning the loss of his son. The Princess walked through the chaos around her and calmly sat down next to him. She picked up a stick nearby and started drawing in the dirt.

The old man noticed her there and looked to see what she was drawing. He recognized the picture, something from long ago, from his son. He didn't question how she knew of it, he just accepted it. After she finished, she turned to him and gently leaned in to whisper. She didn't say a whole lot, but just enough; what he needed to hear.

Meanwhile, the King was trying to regain the attention of the crowd and they were now growing hostile towards him again. He looked at Hope's creatures for answers, but there was no chance to communicate with them because they were also being threatened.

The mob, now picking up stones, started making their way toward the King until, suddenly, someone shouted from within their group.

"Wait!"

It was the old man, now standing, fighting to get their attention. The crowd parted once more and gave him the floor to speak.

"Before my son went off to face King Greedy's army," the old man said addressing everyone, "I pleaded with him not to go. You see...my son could be stubborn," he said with a smile, "a bit like me. So, to convince me, to justify himself...he reminded me of the way things were before. When he was a little lad, we would play a game we called *'King's army.'* He, of course, was always the King. He looked up to you," he said now addressing King Eli, "admired you...he would recite the songs, tell and retell your victories in battle and the peace you brought to the land. But what he was most keen on was your title, '*King Eli, the Common*'. You were like us once. You endured suffering, but you didn't just stand by and shout curses to the wind, or feel sorry for yourself. You made a difference, and my son believed he could do the same. He died years ago, an honorable death. It is fitting that you were the one to let him finally rest in peace. It would have been his honor. He gave his life, inspired by your example. Today, I will not stay idle. I will do as he did...as *you* once did."

Now addressing the crowd, the old man raised his hands and shouted, "Have you not seen with your own eyes and listened to the truth? Hope is still in these lands. Our brothers, our sisters, fathers, mothers, sons and daughters will not have died in vain. If you face them, it will not be as though you hate them, but, out of love, you will give them peace by sending them to the grave. It is not their bodies we are trying to preserve, but their souls."

At this, the crowd cheered and chanted, "We have Hope! We have Hope! We have Hope!"

The old man approached King Eli, placed his hand on his shoulder and said, "I will follow you to the ends of the earth."

"Thank you. We will win these lands back and restore humanity."

"I know."

The old man turned to look at the Princess as she celebrated with the other people.

"She is special, isn't she...your daughter?" he asked the King.

"Yes. How did you know she was my daughter?"

"She has your eyes," he said with a chuckle.

"Should I live long enough to see it, I look forward to the day the Kingdom is under her care and guidance."

Eli smiled and stared at her in awe, cherishing the moment and the light within her.

# Chapter 23

### **Brother**

Joshua traveled a long way.  He had few provisions remaining, so he needed to make a stop at the next village.  Upon arrival, he armed himself.  These were not easy times, especially for a boy his age.

The villagers appeared unresponsive to their surroundings, almost catatonic.  There was no life to be found, nobody *really* living, just simply existing.  The people were downcast and had already accepted death as an invited guest.

Having put away his sword, Joshua walked freely.  There wasn't much there for food.  Whatever happened to be there was rotting away.  He couldn't bring himself to barter for what remained so he gave what little he had to a woman begging in the street.

He continued to survey the village and came across a small child crying. Next to her was a man breathing his last breath. The sight was too much for Joshua. He knelt beside the little girl. He didn't have any words, but he was there so she wouldn't be alone during this moment. The man was gone. She threw her arms around Joshua and they wept together. They were the same; both victims of the cruel world King Greedy created.

Joshua was full of emotions, but none were stronger than anger. He waited patiently for her to finish crying.

"Little one, be not afraid," he told her, "I am your brother now, and you are my sister. What is mine is yours and I will not abandon you. There is hope yet. Do you believe me?"

The little girl nodded in agreement.

"You must wait here. There is something I must do first. Do you trust me?"

Once again, the little girl nodded.

Joshua covered her father with a nearby blanket before marching his way to the center of the village to find the dead soldier keeping watch. As he walked, he pulled his satchel around and removed a bear trap from inside. It was heavy and attached to it was a chain four feet long.

"Hey!" he called to get the soldier's attention.

The dead soldier turned and made eye contact with him.

"Yeah you, baldy!" he shouted as he set the trap on the ground near him.

The onlookers grew tense. One man tried to intervene.

"Boy, what are you doing? Do you want to get us all killed?"

"And what is it you have to live for?" Joshua shouted back.

The man had no answer so Joshua turned his attention once again to the dead soldier. He picked up a smooth stone and threw it, hitting the brute on the head to antagonize it.

The creature drew its sword and quickly advanced toward Joshua. Joshua picked up his trap and started swinging it from its chain. He was focused, calm even, as he waited for the dead soldier to get closer. Once it was in range, Joshua let the trap fly from his hands and it landed directly on the dead soldier's head. There was a loud clamping sound along with the snap its neck, making the kill instant.

The onlookers were amazed. Still, some were confused and scared.

"How is that possible?" they asked him.

"It is. Does it really matter how?" he answered as he collected his weapon from the creature's head. "Now that you have witnessed the truth about them, it is up to you to make a decision. How will you respond? As for me, I will go to the next village and the one after, and the one after that to do what was done just now. Spread the word, arm yourselves, and believe. Maybe you will then remember what it is you have to live for."

Joshua collected the dead soldier's head and placed it in his satchel before he returned to the little girl from before, but she was gone. His heart sank and he wondered what he could have done differently to ensure she was safe.

He turned to leave and there she stood, a donkey to her left and a woman, the same woman begging in the street, standing to her right.

"My daughter told me what you did and what you said…I also witnessed your bravery just now. I heard you. In the small amount of time you've been here, you have been kinder to us and more giving than anyone else since our Kingdom came to ruin. And yet, you are only a boy, but, more so…you are family now. We want you to have our donkey for your journey."

"Oh, no that is too…"

"No, we insist. My husband kept her fed, I admit, much to my dislike, but now I know why. She is strong and will keep you company."

"Thank you kindly."

Joshua strapped his belongings to the donkey and mounted it.

"Before I go, I made promises to my new sister," he said as he smiled at the little girl, "I will be back for you both."

"We believe," the mother said, "there is hope yet."

## Fishers of Men

King Eli, along with the villagers, started battle plans, tactics, and strategies. They needed to do so quickly knowing another dead soldier, perhaps more, would have felt Princess Elise, a first born, enter the land from the forest. In an effort to conceal her, Elise was taken back into the forest along with Hope's creatures to watch over her.

It was time to build an army and the most efficient and sensible way to recruit for a fight against King Greedy would be to use the river. All of the fishermen were called to go and find as many people as they could, people willing to join King Eli's army, men and women alike. They were sent out two by two, with no weapons, only the knowledge they had.

Not everyone would accept their message. People were still afraid and found it difficult to trust the word of men they didn't know and to believe the events they claimed were true. The fishermen expected opposition, so they needed to be tactful in their approach. They couldn't share too much with those remaining skeptical and they needed to be on their guard against people willing to turn them in to King Greedy for a reward. To do this, they started their conversations with lots of questions, enough to examine the hearts of many and to see if they were willing to give their lives to save others.

After visiting with a village and taking a head count for those willing to join King Eli, the fisherman would make a marker on the riverbank indicating the type of response received by the villagers they spoke to. Should the majority of the responses be positive, they would draw a fish parallel to the river. If the message was rejected for the most part, then a fish was drawn perpendicular to the river. The fishermen would do this so when they made their way back to King Eli, they could begin ferrying people from the riverbanks of the villages they knew to stop at.

For those willing to fight but living in a village where the majority was not, they were encouraged by the fisherman to walk over to another place where they knew the majority of the people were like-minded. And for those few untrustworthy and unwilling who lived among many ready to join King Eli, they were kept in the dark about the plans and a close eye was kept on them. Even though they didn't believe it could be done or their hearts seemed too bleak to trust, they were not forgotten. Instead, the believers tried to plant seeds of thoughts and ideas of Hope and the possibilities of fighting together, hoping their faith would increase and would be ready when the time came to fight.

## Enemy of Mankind

The fire which King Greedy set in the forest spread quickly. It was a raging fire, already miles wide, as if the forest was made to burn. The trees were like candle wicks. Even before King Greedy could step out of the forest, he felt the heat from the flames.

There was a mass exodus of animals fleeing away from the danger. Soon, nearby villages were overrun with them. This created a large frenzy, people trying to stake their claim to the fresh meat. Some were dying for their troubles at the hands of hungrier men.

After arriving to his castle, King Greedy was bitter, knowing he lost the upper hand and he blamed King Eli for it. He was not a warrior king as his predecessor, nor was he skilled at fighting or strategizing. Should both kings go to war, King Greedy would inevitably lose. He was smart enough to know this. Still, he only cared about surviving as long as he could and continuing to force upon others the power he acquired. Nothing to him was more rewarding, and he would rather die than see it go to waste. He was a willing enemy of mankind, and he didn't care. He wanted to crush all those inspired by a new belief in the King far greater than himself.

King Greedy prepared for war. By doing so, he first called upon his dead army spread out through all the lands to return to him. Next, he cleared out the surrounding villages, tearing them down and driving out the dwelling scavengers, so he could see all the lands before him. Having a burning forest at his back and clear land in front of him, there would be no surprise attacks. This would be a battle fought head on, his only chance at victory. He was so proud of himself and even felt like a true king because of the superior wisdom he believed he displayed. As his confidence grew, he envisioned himself killing King Eli. He was obsessed with doing so because he was still haunted by the witch's final words.

All the while, the forest fire grew. Smoke was filling the sky, embers gliding on the winds to the farthest corners of the Kingdom. All King Greedy had left to do was wait for King Eli to bring an army of his own. So, every night, King Greedy picked up his fiddle and went up to his balcony overlooking the scorched forest. He would sit and play, watching it all burn.

Joshua

# Chapter 24

### **Confirmation**

Joshua made it to the next village. Upon his arrival, he noticed a crowd gathered in the middle of a courtyard, listening as two men spoke.

"What is going on?" Joshua quietly asked a man near him.

"Something has changed," the man replied. "The dead are abandoning their posts and these men are claiming wild things. They say King Eli lives and is gathering an army...an army of Hope...an army with talking animals! Even if these fantasies were true, the dead cannot be defeated. These men must be drunk and out of their minds!"

There were others in the crowd sharing the same skepticism and the tensions grew. Soon, they were shouting at the two men and were ready to chase them out.

Joshua dismounted from his donkey, forced his way through to stand next to the two men, and drew the attention on himself with a shout.

"Listen to me! I do not know these men or where they come from, but I have traveled from King Greedy's castle where my family and I were once employed. I, alone, have come to know a secret and only a coward would keep it to themselves. With my own eyes, I witnessed one of King Greedy's dead soldiers fall by the sword. I also witnessed a young man murdered by one of the dead soldiers; only, he did not resurrect to become one with them. The natural law of death has found its place in our world again."

The crowd was amazed at what they heard. Still, some needed more proof.

"The power that has protected them is gone,"
Joshua continued. "The power that raised mindless slaves
for King Greedy is no more!"

Joshua reached into his satchel and pulled out the severed
head of the dead soldier he killed with the bear trap.
Immediately, the crowd gasped in awe.

"Look with your own eyes!" Joshua shouted once
more. "Do you still doubt?"

They all knew what he said was true because they
recognized the color of the head to be the same color as
the skin of the dead soldiers; ashen grey. This was one of
their distinct features.

"What should we do?" the crowd asked Joshua.

"Arm yourselves," he answered. "You must
believe that Hope exists, and if there is an army led by
King Eli himself, then you would all be wise to join."

"Follow us," one of the two fishermen interjected towards the crowd, "gather your weapons and provisions. Get your boats ready for we must travel by this river if you want to join King Eli. He and his army await. We don't have any more time to waste."

The crowd dispersed, most going to make preparations to leave their village and join King Eli. Joshua and the two fishermen were left alone to talk.

"Thank you," they told him, "we had been traveling by the river to reach villages in secret. Now with the Dead moving out we do not need to be as subtle as we once were. Still, the water will be the easiest way for all of us to join together. King Eli will be happy to meet you and to hear your report."

"Not just yet," Joshua replied. "I must see and warn the places you have not visited, places farther inland, and tell them the good news I have learned here. As you said, with the dead army now leaving their posts I can freely reach those villages. I will get the word out and gather an army of my own."

"Very well, what is your name?"

"Joshua."

"Then Joshua, we will tell the King about you. Should you need to find us, follow this river south. At some point it will fork, but continue straight. Do not follow the stream left or right. We look forward to fighting alongside you."

Joshua and the fishermen parted ways, now united on their mission.

## **Battle Lines**

Weeks passed. With the Dead having retreated, it was easier to amass an army and gather in one place. With the guidance and wisdom given by Hope's creatures, it was time to go to battle. King Eli, with Princess Elise by his side, stood high above his army to deliver a speech. They were 40, 000 strong.

"Here, before me," he began, "I see a Kingdom unlike any other. I may be your King, but you are not peasants or subjects to me. No, you are more. You are family.

There was a time when I forgot what that was: family. For eight years, I was lost in the forest under the power of the witch. I should have died, but Hope intervened and saved me. He didn't just save me; he helped restore my mind and reminded me why I needed to keep fighting.

With his guidance, we defeated the witch, lifted her curse, and rescued my daughter. I had to endure much suffering and torment because I made a selfish decision, and that will not happen again.

Look around you. These are your brothers and sisters, mothers, fathers, sons, and daughters. You will no longer fight each other just to survive, but you will give your life, lay it down with the intention of saving the life next to you.

Men and women, young and old, this is your fight. Our strength comes from our reverence and love for one another, the driving force of hope. And do not let the size of their army deceive you; fear is not stronger than hope. *This* is our greatest weapon against our enemy."

The King took a moment and examined the brave army.

"This is the end," the King spoke once more, "the end of pestilence and the beginning of light. It is in our grasp! So, let us fight together, united as one!"

The army cheered and yelled out their battle cries, ready to give their all.

### In the Middle of the Fight

Immediately after his speech, Princess Elise tugged at his sleeve.

"And what shall I do?" she asked.

"We must keep you hidden and safe," he replied. "Perhaps you can stay here with the others that are unable to fight. We can leave a group of soldiers just in case."

"Now, you mustn't do that," the rabbit spoke up. "The Princess has been out of the forest for some time now. The dead soldiers already know she is here. We can't risk her staying and endangering, not only her life, but the lives of all that are to remain. It would also be unwise to pull able bodied soldiers away from the fight. Our force needs to be at its strongest."

"What about the forest? What if we hide her in there?" The King asked now feeling a sense of desperation to keep his daughter safe.

"You know very well, it is just as dangerous there. The fire has almost completely covered it. She would have to evacuate in a day's time."

"Then what do you propose? That she comes with us?"

"Yes."

"Yes!? Take her to the fight? I need to protect her. I'm surprised you'd make such a suggestion."

"You are speaking as a father just reunited with his daughter after eight years, so I understand you are upset, but you are also being led by your fear, which is the absence of hope. If you lack the courage, many more lives will be lost."

Although he did not want to hear it, King Eli knew the rabbit was right. It didn't matter where she was, she would still be in danger.

"It is only a matter of time before they come looking for her," the rabbit spoke again. "It doesn't matter if they were all summoned to the castle, there will be a few of the Dead that sense her and will come. This will happen no matter where she is. As we fight, unless commanded specifically, they will ignore her and face the threats in front of them. Their first obligation is to protect their king. Let her come. We will surround her, protect her on all sides."

"Very well," the King agreed reluctantly. King Eli turned to the Princess to reassure her.

"This is where you need to be, with us," he told her.

"I understand father. I am not afraid. If this is what you ask of me, then so be it."

No matter how many times he saw it, King Eli was always impressed by his daughter. He didn't understand how she got to be so wise and fearless for her age.

# Chapter 25

## **Two Kings go to War**

King Eli's army marched a day before arriving to the battlefield. Upon arriving, they were armed and ready to fight their oppressor. The day was dark and overcast with the whole forest was now completely in flames; ash and embers were floating all over the land and the heat given off was immense. Should someone stand too close, it would kill them.

King Greedy's dead army stood shoulder to shoulder, all 80,000. Far behind them stood their master high above on a wooded platform he had constructed for the occasion. He wanted to witness the battle, his defining moment as king.

The battle began. There were no words exchanged. With King Eli leading the way in front, his army started slowly, gradually building speed until they were in a full-on charge. The King was like a madman as he tore through the dead army. He fought with ferocity and skill. There was a fluidity in his attack; countering and attacking at the same time.

The battle cries were loud as many were dropping quickly on both sides. The Princess and Miriam were both riding bears, swords in hand, striking down any of the Dead managing to get close enough. They roared alongside their animal companions, a sleuth of 12 total.

The clash was fierce; men and women of all ages gave their lives. Many of the elderly carried a crossbow with one shot. They were warriors with limitations, but warriors none the less, and were just as important to the cause as their younger counterparts. Upon firing their one shot, a kill shot, all they could do next was throw up their hands, surrendered to their fate as the next dead soldier went in to kill them.

King Eli's army was greatly outnumbered and his men were beginning to lose heart when suddenly they heard trumpets blasting. It was Joshua. He had with him a small army of his own, 10,000 strong; men and women eager to change the fate of their children and the future of the Kingdom.

Watching as Joshua joined the fight, King Greedy shuttered. Once again, he was struck with fear and he didn't have anywhere he could run. The fighting was now all around him and the forest was burning endlessly behind.

With Joshua joining the fray, there was renewed strength and hope in King Eli's army. The added adrenaline helped them push forward towards victory.

King Eli found himself a stone's throw away from where King Greedy stood. He charged ahead taking out several more of the Dead before he finally reached the twenty-foot-high perch.

"It is finished!" King Eli yelled up to King Greedy.

"Perhaps, but my fall will come at a great cost to you!"

King Greedy kept two of the dead soldiers by his side. He turned to one and whispered. Suddenly, all of the dead army ignored the fighting men in front of them and began running past, as if fleeing. King Eli's army believed this to be the case because they desperately wanted the fighting to end, so they started to celebrate prematurely.

From his vantage point, however, King Eli knew what was happening. He could see the dead army making their way all at once and without much resistance, toward Princess Elise.

"No!" King Eli shouted in vain, "Protect the Princess!"

It was too late for a strong response, but Joshua noticed the shift in the battle, and was not as eager to celebrate. He knew something was wrong so he ran faster than the dead army, ahead in the direction they were going until he found his way to the Princess. He didn't completely understand, seeing a young girl riding a bear and now surrounded by the dead army. Still, he didn't hesitate. He rushed over and began fighting alongside the bears to keep her safe.

"You will lose no matter what," King Eli said, trying to reason with King Greedy.

"Yes, I anticipate that. At least I'll die knowing *you* will still lose and suffer for it," he said while laughing.

"Then have me instead," the King shouted. "Spare my daughter and I will give up right now, but call them off."

King Greedy was flattered by the proposal and whispered into his guard's ear once more.

The dead army swarmed and were overwhelming. During the skirmish, Elise was knocked off her bear and quickly grabbed by a dead soldier, when suddenly, the dead army stopped their fighting and spoke in unison.

"Stop! It is over. We will not fight. Your King has offered to sacrifice himself for all of you. I will surrender after his death, I only wish for an audience," King Greedy said through them. "There doesn't need to be anymore death. You will all be able to go home to your loved ones…victorious. Now please, direct your attention to me and witness the death of your King."

Since the men and women in battle were eager to end the fight, some were relieved by what was announced. Still, many didn't trust King Greedy.

"Should you continue to fight, I will take back my little arrangement and you will all risk the death of many more of your friends, starting with the Princess here. As a sign of my pledge I have commanded my army to refrain from battle…for now. But we will hold on to the girl just in case."

At once, the Dead retreated to reposition themselves surrounding King Greedy. This was a good enough sign for the fighting to come to an end. At this, King Eli surrendered himself.

## Master's Voice
All eyes were on King Greedy atop his perch. Below him was King Eli, bound in ropes, dead soldiers on all sides.

"That's right!" King Greedy shouted out, "Look at your King now!"

A noose was quickly thrown around his neck and he was instantly hoisted up into the air, high enough for all to see.

"King Eli, in all of his glory!" King Greedy mocked.

King Eli struggled as he hung, but he was able to see Princess Elise. She was sobbing. Others gathered around trying to convince her to look away. All Eli wanted in this moment was to hold her one last time. He was full of regret. With only one chance at being a parent, he missed out and blamed himself for the torment Elise had to endure. Now, he was going to leave her alone, again.

The seconds passing seemed a lifetime for him. He was having visions of his past, happier days with his wife. The nights they dreamed of having a large family together, a time of peace and hope. His vision started to blur and he accepted his fate as he was quickly losing consciousness. Then it happened again. Like all the other times before, he heard the all too familiar voice in an unlikely moment.

"Down he goes, let him down."
Suddenly, the dead soldiers released the rope and King Eli went crashing to the floor, gasping for the air to return to his lungs, sucking for life to re-enter his body.

"What is this?!" King Greedy demanded. He turned only to see the witch making her way through the crowd of dead soldiers, clasping the wound he gave her; blood oozing out between her fingers.

"You should be dead!" he shouted in horror.

"Not by your hand, never by you," the old witch replied.

"Kill her!" King Greedy ordered his army.

They didn't move.

"What is wrong with you?  Do you not hear my voice?"

"They know their master's voice: me, not you, never you."

The Princess made her way through the crowd, along with Joshua and Miriam, to help King Eli out of the ropes and noose binding him.

Now enraged, King Greedy grabbed a sword, climbed off his perch and moved to strike the witch.  He didn't get very far.  He was immediately grabbed by the dead soldiers.

"Greedy in life, greedy to death," the witch told him.

The dead soldiers took the noose once destined to kill King Eli and secured King Greedy with it.  All at once the remaining thousands of dead soldiers made their way toward the burning forest. One by one, they entered. The two dead soldiers King Greedy had grown accustomed to keeping by his side during his reign were now dragging him to the fire. He was kicking and screaming, crying out for pity and mercy, but it was no use. He was taken into the flames and was no more.

With the dark army now vanquished and King Greedy dead, only the witch remained for all to see. She stood silently. The people were tense, expecting her to give them her worst, but she only stood there. Her veil removed. Her milky white eyes were staring out as if she could see them all. For a moment, it was as though her eyes fixed on someone before finally turning around to make her way back into the burning forest.

"Wait," King Eli called out, "is this it? Is it over?"

"I am not needed right now, not yet. Not too long for me, others like Greedy Fool to be," she said without stopping or looking back.

She walked slowly, but eventually made her way into the fiery flames.

## In Good Company

King Eli's army cheered and celebrated at the top of their voices. King Greedy's eight-year reign of horror was over. Still, King Eli wasn't satisfied, he had to know what the witch meant by what she said. The rabbit stood by him and, knowing the questions he had, answered them.

"There will be others like Greedy Fool. The truth is: the witch isn't needed to make the world a dark place. She just knows how to speed up the process."

"There are plenty of good people here."

"Yes, and more than enough not so good. The human race isn't perfect. She knows this and she loves to exploit the imperfections."

"Will she come back?"

"Maybe someday…maybe in a different form…maybe no form at all."

"Why can she not be destroyed? Shouldn't you just kill her once and for all?"

"There is a time and place. Still, you've changed things, or rather, your daughter, the Princess, did. The witch doesn't have the power she once possessed, but that will not stop her from trying to influence people to bring darkness into the world; the kind she craves. Men have a choice: choose darkness or light. Your daughter will bring a brighter light than the world has ever seen."

"And what about you? Your home is gone. Where will you go?"

"Once again, your daughter changed things. My home wasn't in the forest. Those are things you may never understand. Perhaps my home will be in the wind, or we'll take to the skies. My time has come to leave the animals be. You and your family will now become my messengers. You must go and spread hope and love throughout all the lands. Get ahead of the darkness, restore and rebuild people's faith."

"What of my daughter? Can you at least tell me what will come in her lifetime? Will she face men like Greedy Fool?"

"There will be peace in her lifetime, you need not worry."
They both paused to look over to see her and Joshua celebrating together.

"She will be in good company," the rabbit continued. "She will live a long and fulfilling life. It will not be until she is gone and her child takes the throne will there be the beginnings of unrest; later generations out of touch with the events of these last eight years and grow accustomed to loving the darkness…but even in darkness there is always Hope."

King Eli took a moment to reflect on what he heard.

"Rejoice, King! You did it!" the rabbit told him, "You've restored your honor, saved your Kingdom, and now united with your daughter."

"Thank you," King Eli replied, "without your help, all would be lost. I will make sure everyone knows to tell the stories of Hope."

The King finally smiled and joined the celebration, and the whole Kingdom rejoiced.

# Chapter 26

### **Establishing Hope**

It took the Kingdom another eight years to finish rebuilding and restoring order. The lands were brought back to all of their glory; rich soil yielding fruitful crops and the people were united.

During this time, King Eli traveled far and wide to spread the good news of their victory, re-establish trust, and bring a message of Hope. Along for the journey was Princess Elise. It was important for the people to become familiar with their future Queen and it didn't take long for news to spread about her. She was loved and well received. People felt a sense of calm when they met her. Even those who were most skeptical, due to their hurt and suffering, came to adore her.

King Eli kept his word in telling all the people

about Hope and the victory he brought about. He also testified to how Hope changed his life and saved him. Still, it was Princess Elise's idea to build monuments in Hope's honor, to include the testimonies of those most impacted by him, along with the stories of the great triumph over evil. They knew without Hope, the world would be doomed.

The people were greatly influenced by the mission of the King and Princess. So much so, they started writing and singing songs of Hope. People would gather around the monuments to sing and celebrate during festivals created to commemorate the victory. Hope was well received and was even given different names. But what the people mostly associated him with was love.

This wasn't all King Eli set out to do. He relished the opportunity to travel the world and spend as much time with his daughter as possible. For him, their travels to introduce Elise to the people were more of an excuse to spend time with her. Being King and securing the future of the Kingdom was always second and much less important to him than his role as a father.

It was important to King Eli to have a mother figure in Princess Elise's life. He appointed Miriam as Royal Mother. She had a high standing within the Kingdom, and was by all intents and purposes, the Queen, simply without the title and marriage to the King.

Joshua reunited with his father and brother. He also kept his promise going back for the woman and her daughter he met during his travels. This was his family and they were well taken care of. Joshua became King Eli's most trusted ally and pupil. He was mentored to govern the people and make decisions for the good of the Kingdom. On many occasions, when the King and

Princess were at home in the castle and not traveling, Joshua and his family were welcomed guests.

After eight years, all was right in the Kingdom. There was a new light guiding the world, and there was peace. For eight years, King Eli was a father. This relationship helped him remember how to love. He and Elise grew close and seemed inseparable. He could see her growing into a great Queen right before his eyes. She was after all, just like her mother.

## **Tree of Life**

King Eli stood alone above his balcony staring out at the peaceful Kingdom as the world slept. The moon was full and bright.

"Thank you," he whispered.

The weary King went to his bed and laid down on the right side for one last time.

This is what he dreamt:

The King opened his eyes and found himself standing at the entrance of a beautiful garden. It was alive with magnificent colors, strange but elegant flowers, and spirited creatures enjoying their paradise.

Eli walked around and enjoyed the scenery. He noticed footprints just ahead. They were imbedded in the ground and somehow, he knew they were there waiting for him, welcoming him. They walked the trail together, side by side. The presence of the footprints was comforting. He felt as if the weight of the world had been lifted.

Finally, the path the King and his companion were walking ended at an expanse of green land. At the center of this land was a massive tree unlike any other. None could match its beauty. All kinds of fruits were thriving and many creatures and birds made their home in and around it. The Kingdom was built around this tree.

The footprints walked ahead leading Eli around the tree's base, which was a good walk due to its immensity. Eventually, Eli was led to a very large mirror, ten feet high and ten feet wide. The footprints, still ahead, waited for him standing directly in front of it. He slowly peaked his head over, but didn't see himself in the reflection. Instead, he saw *her*. Sarai, his wife, was waiting for him, smiling. Upon seeing her, he felt his knees buckle just a bit.

"There he is," she said, "the man I married."

Eli hesitated.

"I'm...I'm sorry," he told her gently. It was all he could think to say.

"You don't need to be. I forgave you a long time ago."

He paused for a moment, grateful to hear those words.

"Did you see our daughter?" he asked.

"Yes, she is beautiful and strong."

"Just like her mother."

"I agree," she said still smiling and with a little laugh.

"It seems like only yesterday we were two kids hiding in a wine press...oh, how I've missed you," he said now in tears.

"And I, you."

King Eli would have looked one last time at his Kingdom before joining the Queen, but he was different. He didn't need to be King, nor did he desire to have his own Kingdom. All he ever wanted was right in front of him. The thought of looking back never crossed his mind.

"I'm ready," he said.

Sarai took a step forward and reached out with her hand passing through the mirror. Eli held it tight and crossed over to join her forever.

After having endured so much pain and unrest, King Eli clung to hope. And having undergone total transformation, he found salvation through love…because hope would not be possible without it.

The End

## From the Author

The idea for this story came to me when I was sitting in my Art History class at the University of Houston. I was doodling, as I often did, on the outside margins of my notes. I had recently saw *the Ring* and wanted to draw that little creepy girl coming out of the well.

I messed around a bit with her face and out of this strange picture I envisioned my new creation to be a Princess. Soon I was lost in my thoughts creating a back story for this single sketch.

I had MANY ideas and I loved to brainstorm during my six hour drives to visit my family in San Benito, TX. This went on for EIGHT YEARS! It finally took a phone conversation with my brother Brian that I decided it was time to put my thoughts to paper. Even as I wrote the story changed, as I'm sure it often does for many writers. I wanted to make a different kind of fairy tale and as I went to work and read back the story in my head, I would envision reading it to my daughter.

What I knew for certain out of every idea I had, the story would simply be called *SHUTT*. I'll be honest, I didn't really know why at the time. It made little sense. Why two T's? I'd often ask myself. I didn't want to force it either, but while writing the first few chapters, I knew where my story was going to end up. Then it hit me: *Salvation Having Undergone Total Transformation*.

This story is a journey, the King's journey to be more specific. Here is a man that had what he wanted in life until it was ripped from him. He was faced with a decision and he gave up on hope. This changed his life forever. Eli stared at himself many days and yet he didn't know the man he was looking at. It would take deep soul searching to become the man he once was; the kind of father Elise needed and the husband Sarai fell in love with.

So, thank you for taking this journey with me! I hope it resonates with you in some way. If not, well I hope you simply enjoyed it.


Cody F. Fonseca


Twitter: @SHUTT_Fonseca
www.facebook.com/SHUTTbook
shuttbook@yahoo.com

342

Made in United States
Orlando, FL
01 December 2023